HOUNDED

E.J. Cochrane

**Other Bella Books by
E.J. Cochrane**

Matilda Smithwick Mystery Series
Sleeping Dogs Lie
Double Dog Dare

About the Author

E.J. Cochrane is a native Chicagoan currently on loan to Indianapolis. She taught college English for fifteen years before calling it quits, and now she has a much less stressful job in retail. She's also worked numerous odd jobs, including operating her own dog walking business (which, fortunately, did not involve moonlighting as an amateur sleuth). In addition to writing and retail, she's also an allegedly retired marathoner who still enjoys running, even without the promise of a finisher's medal. She and her partner share their home with a ball-obsessed pit bull and four needy cats.

HOUNDED

E.J. Cochrane

BELLA BOOKS

2023

Acknowledgments

The inspiration for this mystery sprang from my decades-long love for the movie *Clue*, but turning obsession into the book you're now holding was a tremendous group effort. As always, my sister, Jennie Tyderek, and my partner, Sue Hawks, offered just the right blend of loving support and assertive nudging to get me across the finish line. From brainstorming to fashion consultation to alpha reading to self-doubt taming, they both came to my rescue repeatedly, and for that I thank you, I love you, and I need you to rest up for the next book. Tremendous thanks also to my dear friend Patrick Doyle—your culinary expertise is always appreciated. I'm sorry for destroying your work. To my beta readers, Lynda Fitzgerald, Diane Piña, Amy Cook, Kathy Rowe and Heather L. Mathes, your attention to detail and adherence to the rules of logic have made this a much more delightful book. Thank you for making Maddie a better sleuth. Huge thanks to Ann Roberts, the greatest editor on the planet, for all of your help and support. Finally, thanks to everyone at Bella for doing all the hard work. I'm proud to put my books in your hands.

Dedication

For Bart, who set the Good Dog bar impossibly high. And for Gonzo, who doesn't even care that it exists.

Cast of Characters

Matilda "Maddie" Smithwick: Owner of Little Guys Pet Care, accidental detective.

Gwendolyn "Dottie" Hunter: Fashion maven, strategic spouse, Maddie's best friend.

Carlisle: Dottie's hyper-efficient assistant.

Jason Van Dam: Entertainer, Dottie's love interest.

Rebecca Douglas: Jason's little sister.

Cate Bennet: Cosmetics mogul.

Florence Saldana: COO of Andreas Corporation.

Eric Dillingham: Horse-loving billionaire.

Castor Andreas: Spoiled socialite, Helen's twin brother, Ares's dad.

Helen Andreas: Castor's twin, Florence's boss, Dottie's competition.

Mammon and Archer: Resident guard dogs.

Ares: Castor's Yorkipoo.

PROLOGUE

Helen Andreas descended the wine cellar stairs to enjoy a much-needed moment of peace. As usual, she tripped on the uneven stair at the bottom and made a mental note to remind her resident handyman to fix it once this horrid weekend was over. Rather than fumbling to find the switch for the wall sconces (another fix for the handyman), she lit a candle and enjoyed the gothic appeal of the space. It was almost like being in Poe's "The Cask of Amontillado," if Montressor's wine cellar had been appointed with perfect climate control, a cozy seating area and one of the finest private wine collections on the East Coast.

This was the one area of her mansion that she had declared off-limits to the guests (not *her* guests as she'd been reminded throughout the day) currently occupying her property, and she intended to enjoy the solitude, at least until her scarcely welcome appointment intruded upon her serenity. She didn't know why she'd agreed to this meeting—a moment of weakness perhaps—but she intended to get it over with quickly. She'd been around these people less than a day, and she was already tired of them asking for things she didn't want to give. Every time she turned around, she faced another demand for money, leniency, privacy, or distance. At this point, regardless of what anyone requested of her, she was determined to say no. The allure, she supposed, was in the art of the refusal—how would she do it this time? Would she lift this leech's spirits first? Would she be merciful and deny their requests before they got their hopes up? Maybe she would toy with the beggar, give the impression that she might be swayed before issuing her rejection. There had to be some way to spice up the monotony of these endless appeals.

It had been a particularly trying day, starting with her brother's regularly scheduled plea for money (and the dull throb of a headache that he had induced) and ending with watching her beloved Jason fall under Gwendolyn Hunter's mystifying spell. Personally, she didn't understand the sway that woman had over men, but she had to applaud its efficacy. To her knowledge, Gwendolyn hadn't worked a day in the last decade, yet she had amassed a fortune that Castor would kill for, though Helen doubted that her shiftless brother would put forth even that minimal effort when he could simply whine or wheedle his way into some cash. Truth be told, it was exceptionally gratifying to watch Gwendolyn rebuff Castor's sad attempts at gold digging the queen of gold diggers.

"If she wasn't competition for Jason's affections, I'd happily toast her success." Helen laughed bitterly.

Perusing her impressive selection of wine, she admired her own considerable gift for amassing wealth. True, she'd had the advantage of exceptionally rich parents, but she'd taken the empire they'd built and expanded it beyond their limited expectations. Her parents had been so pleased with themselves for personifying the cliché of the immigrant who made it big that they had settled for success in their one small corner of the market. They hadn't even considered branching out until she took over. Now, she sat at the top of Andreas Corporation, overseeing the many avenues the company had expanded into, and for the most part, dominated.

Feeling particularly indulgent, she grabbed the bottle of Château Cheval Blanc 1947 that she'd dropped over a quarter of a million on. Settling at the small table in the center of the room, she poured a glass and allowed herself to relax for the first time since she'd arrived that afternoon, though flashes of her many ordeals that day disrupted the peace she strove for. That fight with that idiot horse lover Eric hadn't helped her mood any. What business of his was it how she wanted to spend her money? If she wanted to set fire to a million dollars cash, it wasn't his concern.

"Pompous ass," she muttered. "It'll be a miracle if we both survive this weekend."

She'd wanted to smack his weak-chinned face, but Jason had chosen that moment to acknowledge her existence, so she had to be on her best, most alluring behavior. That Eric had looked equally ready to resort to violence had also given her pause (not that she'd let him know as much).

It stung, too, that Florence had been visibly disappointed to see her. She knew she was a demanding boss, but she also rewarded ingenuity and loyalty, something Florence would do well to remember. Perhaps she should issue a reminder, maybe in the form of a pointed question about her ailing mother, whose status in this country was questionable at best. She wouldn't actually do anything to hurt the woman—she was in her eighties for the love of god—but it didn't hurt for Florence to believe that her mother's well-being was in peril.

She took a moment to savor her wine, appreciating not just its porty richness but also the fact that, unlike so many, she could easily afford such an indulgence. After one sip, she could pour the rest down the drain or pass the bottle off to the world's luckiest vagabond if she chose (not that she was likely to find a pauper on her private island). She wouldn't miss it or the money she'd spent, but what fun it would be to do so while her idiot brother watched the wealth he longed for thrown so casually away. The racks that lined the stone walls of her wine cellar were crowded with equally impressive (and equally disposable) vintages. And she didn't even particularly care for wine, not like Castor did.

Suddenly, she was blasted in artificial light, and she turned at the sound of footsteps on the stairs behind her. "You're early. I wasn't expecting you for—what are *you* doing here?" She didn't have the time or patience for this distraction.

"I want to talk to you."

"Let me guess, you think I'm being cruel and unfair and that I should reconsider."

"As a matter of fact, I do." Her surprise guest stepped closer—too close—anger flashing in the eyes that met hers.

"That makes one of us." Already bored by this unexpected intrusion on her privacy, she turned her attention back to the deep red liquid in her glass.

"You're going to listen to me whether you like it or not."

A hand on her shoulder spun her roughly around, sending her glass crashing to the cobblestone floor.

"Do you honestly believe you'll get what you want by attacking me?"

"No. I don't believe you'll ever willingly give me what I want. The only way is for me to take it." A chill ran through her at the sound of the cold, emotionless voice just as her visitor's hands closed around her throat.

CHAPTER ONE

Six hours earlier

Matilda Smithwick cursed the full-length mirror that showed her just how ludicrous she looked. The dress she'd donned under protest—the one Dottie swore would transform her outlook on fashion—looked like a crocheted hot air balloon. Apparently, the hip, up-and-coming designer (whose name Maddie had willfully forgotten) was unaware that women's bodies were not pyramid-shaped. Or perhaps she was paid by the hectare. There was just so much fabric. God forbid she got caught in a strong wind. Feeling the stirrings of an apparel-based headache, she rubbed her temples, cringing at the thunderous rustling of her puffy sleeves. She frowned at her reflection, wondering how she had gotten into this sartorial nightmare, and more importantly, how she would get out of it.

"It's exquisite," Dottie gasped, and Maddie turned to find her much-less-ostentatiously clad friend holding a cocktail in each hand and eyeing her critically. She genuinely feared the next stage of her transformation at Dottie's hands. "Turn for me. I want to see it in all its glory."

Maddie grabbed the liquid fortification that would get her through this evening and obediently made a circle, lamenting the moment of weakness that had led her to agree to this absurd outing.

The previous evening, at the end of a spectacularly grueling day, she'd wanted nothing more than to hide under the covers with her dogs and a good book. That hope vanished the second Dottie swooped into her living room, poured them both drinks and declared that they would be going away for the weekend.

"Nice of you to ask, but—"

"We're going, apple platz. No arguments. I intend to whisk you away from the stressors in your life before those wrinkles become permanent." Unconsciously, Maddie touched her forehead. "And it just so happens that your impending breakdown and my birthday celebration coincide."

"I took you out to dinner for your birthday when it happened, in January."

"And don't think I didn't appreciate that adorable little bistro. This celebration is in honor of my quarter birthday."

"It was a four-star restaurant," she said, ignoring the more perplexing issue of the quarter birthday and why it invoked travel.

"Carlisle and I have everything planned and ready to go. You just need to grab your toothbrush and your sense of adventure." Dottie paused to scrutinize her. "Maybe throw some hair care products in the mix."

"I wish I could help you celebrate this momentous occasion, but I can't leave town right now. I'm in the middle of moving my business, which is busier than ever."

"What's to move? The milk-bone buffet and a year's supply of poop bags? Besides, your father assured me that the new space won't be ready for a few more weeks."

"You talked to my father?"

"He sends his regards. As for the business, Patrick has everything under control."

"Of course he does," she grumbled, bemoaning her assistant's efficiency and eagerness to help. "But I can't just leave Bart and Goliath here by themselves."

"Obviously not, fruit cup. Thankfully, your incomparable grandmother has agreed to tend to your beasts while we're away."

"You just assume I'm free?"

"Oh, petunia." Dottie offered her most pitying expression. "We both know you don't have any dates to cancel or a girlfriend you need to ask for permission." Maddie scowled at the reminder that she was habitually alone. "One rocky relationship's demise is not cause for eternal sorrow, and your mourning period has now outlasted the relationship that inspired it. You need to get out and have fun, and lucky you, your best friend is here to save the day."

"With a party in her honor."

"Not a party, sheepskin. An extravaganza. I've rented a mansion and the private island it occupies."

"The Taj Mahal wasn't available? Why would you rent an island?"

"I would have bought it, but the owner is unreasonable."

"How dare they not uproot their entire lives to accommodate your party needs," Maddie scoffed.

"Be serious, Matilda. Helen rarely visits the property. She merely holds onto it as a status symbol, one she was all too happy to profit from. Alas, no sum of money could prevent her from inviting herself to join us." A monumental frown punctuated Dottie's statement.

"That hardly sounds like the relaxing weekend you think I need."

"Not to worry, little one. With any luck, Helen's plane will crash and the world will be a better place."

Maddie shook her head in disbelief, but in spite of herself, she was warming to this idea. It wasn't like she had anything better to do that weekend. Or any weekend ever.

"We leave frightfully early tomorrow. Be ready to go by eleven." Dottie emptied her glass with a flourish and turned toward the door.

"To go where?" Maddie refrained from pointing out how much the opposite of "frightfully early" eleven was.

"It's a surprise, dumpling."

"How will I know what to pack?"

"I wouldn't expect you to pack appropriate attire if I gave you a checklist and the precise coordinates of our destination. Just throw your sad, tired jeans and T-shirts in whatever you have that passes for luggage, and I'll make sure you have something to wear to my parties."

And with that she'd sauntered out of the house, leaving Maddie in a wake of confusion and apprehension—a surprise trip to a mystery destination with Dottie in control of her wardrobe. She hadn't even bothered to tempt fate by asking what could possibly go wrong. Evidently the fates needed no such provocation because now here she stood, wearing the world's largest doily and wishing it came with a bag to put over her head.

"Is this really necessary? Your friends aren't here for me. Can't I just hide in the corner?"

"Sorry, ducks. I can't allow my best friend to lurk on the sidelines for this auspicious event."

"I'm less likely to hide if I don't have to wear this." She gestured to her voluminous skirt. "I look like a pup tent."

Dottie lifted one elegantly sculpted eyebrow. "I know you'd rather stomp around in your rustic finest, Grizzly Adams, but this is an important night for me. Flannel and combat boots won't cut it."

"I just want to wear pants to dinner. It's not like I'm trying to resurrect grunge."

"It's not much better."

"But if I wear this…masterpiece, then all eyes will be on me. You don't want me stealing the spotlight, do you?"

"Sweetie, it's a dress, not a magic trick."

"So, if I'm destined to be overshadowed by you, do my clothes really matter?" Dottie gasped in horror. "I'm merely suggesting that, instead of making me even more self-conscious than necessary with this dress, I could wear something a little more me."

"I suppose you may have a point."

Dottie moved to the closet, which Maddie had completely missed in her initial perusal of the room. As she'd expected from a Dottie-sponsored outing, her accommodations were both comfortable and commodious, if somewhat questionably decorated. On the walk from the foyer to her third-floor bedroom, Maddie had spied myriad portraits (each in a gilded frame more garish than the last), scores of ornamental vases (the pronunciation of which had to be "vahz," she could tell just by looking at them) and an abundance of statuary in every form from cherubic to representatives from the animal kingdom. One such monstrosity sat in the corner of Maddie's room—an owl the size of a third-grade child, staring judgmentally at the bed. She couldn't help but wonder if the interior designer had consulted Liberace via séance for tips.

Maddie's bedroom was one of thirteen in the sprawling mansion that held the distinction of being the only home on this island off the picturesque coast of Maine. And while the queen-size bed, with its ultra-soft leopard-print comforter and multitude of pillows, had her longing for bedtime, even that splendor was eclipsed by the view from her balcony. She hadn't hesitated to throw open the French doors and drink in the spectacular scenery. From that vantage, she could see not only the outlying guesthouse, boathouse, stables and teahouse (whatever that was) but also the surrounding woods. She'd been so distracted by the beautifully dense foliage between them and the ocean that she'd completely missed the black garment bags that hung (somewhat ominously) in the walk-in closet from which Dottie now emerged, Maddie's designer destiny in her hands.

"Tonight, you can wear this dress." She unzipped the garment bag to reveal a black cocktail dress that, by all appearances, was in no way outrageous or daring. Maddie might even have considered buying it herself (if her clothing allowance sat nearer to Kim Kardashian's than Kimmy Schmidt's). Halfway through Maddie's sigh of relief, Dottie unveiled a pair of black heels that were closer to the stilt family than to shoes. "But you'll also have to wear these."

Maddie backed away as if the shoes were venomous. "You know that heels and I don't mix."

"You just need more experience."

"And you think this is the proper venue?"

"It's these or the other dress."

Maddie carefully weighed her options, preferring neither of them. "Remind me who I'll have to face tonight."

"I really should congratulate myself on the guest list. Paragons of society, every single one." Maddie savored the eye roll that followed her best friend's entire lack of humility. "For starters, Cate Bennet will be in attendance." Dottie spoke Cate's name in reverent tones, the inspiration for which eluded Maddie. "She's only the gatekeeper of the Midwest's most spectacular fall fashion gala, an event to which I'm sure to secure an invitation as a repayment for the undeniably tasteful elegance of this weekend."

"If that doesn't do the trick, I'm sure your modesty will."

"Cate's also a cosmetics demigod, so we'll have to do something with your face," she added with an ominous grin. "We'll also be joined by Florence Saldana. I've known her since my second marriage when she was merely a pill-pushing pharmaceutical sales rep, but now she's the COO of the number two drug company in the nation. She desperately needs time away from her ogre of a boss, so I have graciously come to her rescue."

"How magnanimous of you," Maddie deadpanned.

"Plus she's one of your people, so you'll get along famously."

"Yes, because all lesbians are besties." Deciding that perilous footwear was marginally more palatable than a parachute for a dress, Maddie reluctantly slipped into option number two.

"Well, you'll have something in common with my friend Eric Dillingham. He's an animal lover through and through. True, his passion lies in the equestrian, not the canine, realm, but he funds several animal charities."

That sounded promising, or at least as promising as any of Dottie's wealthy connections could be, but the guest list was feeling fairly tycoon heavy. "Am I going to know anyone other than you?"

"Castor Andreas is coming—you've walked his Yorkipoo, Ares. He's a terrible flirt and a complete gold digger, but he's entertaining, and he could be worthwhile insurance."

"For?" She struggled with her zipper a moment before Dottie came to the rescue.

"For Jason." She laid a well-manicured hand on her surgically enhanced bosom. "An entertainment mogul—you know how I've been thinking of branching out into that arena." Maddie knew no such thing but opted not to admit that. "He's the apotheosis of masculinity, and as wealthy as he is gorgeous. I'm still in the wooing phase, so it's vital that you make a good impression on him, especially if I can parlay Castor's flirting into a proposal from Jason."

"He's the next Mr. Dottie?"

"If all goes well." She had a calculated look in her eye. "And I have planned meticulously for all to go extremely well. Do not embarrass me in front of Jason."

"That would be easier if I didn't have to attempt walking in heels."

"If you cared about me at all, you would refine your heel-walking skills."

"I'll put it on my to-do list," she deadpanned and immediately lost her balance. "Will I be the only representative from the middle class?"

"Jason is bringing his younger sister. I believe she's closer to your tax bracket. And she's also of your persuasion." Dottie's accompanying wink held zero subtlety.

"How nice for both of us."

"I've completed the inventory of the property, including photographs," Carlisle announced upon entering the room.

"Wonderful, Carlisle. The last thing I need is Helen accusing me of damaging one of her démodé couches or ghastly portraits." She lounged on Maddie's bed, the preponderance of decorative pillows encroaching upon her space. "And has everyone made it to the island safely?"

"The last of the guests have arrived and are in their rooms freshening up for dinner." Carlisle frowned and looked at her feet before adding, "Except for Ms. Andreas."

Dottie's eyebrows flew to astronomical heights. "I didn't invite Ms. Andreas."

"She insisted that she's welcome."

"A gross exaggeration of the facts. Did you try to get rid of her?"

"I did."

"And?"

"She threatened to sic the dogs on us."

"Has she met the dogs?" Maddie asked, reflecting on her introduction to Mammon and Archer, the bullmastiffs tasked with protecting the island, and their resident handler, Timothy.

Maddie, Dottie, and Carlisle had been on the property less than five minutes before roughly two hundred pounds of dog bounded toward them, their jowls flapping as they ran. They certainly looked the part of security dogs as their well-muscled, oversize bodies charged toward the interlopers, but the similarity ended there. Mammon, the slightly smaller fawn-colored female, dropped to the ground at Maddie's feet and rolled onto her back, exposing her belly for rubs while her brindle brother focused his attention on an apparently threatening stick. For good reason, Maddie questioned the magnitude of Helen's threat, but she seemed to be in the minority.

"This is an unmitigated disaster." Dottie downed both her drink and Maddie's before turning toward the door. "I have to welcome my newest guest, poppy seed. I expect to see you downstairs in twenty minutes. Do not be late."

CHAPTER TWO

Maddie hardly contained her moan of delight when she took her place at the dinner table ninety minutes later. Sitting was beyond pleasurable, and the relief her aching feet felt in that moment was on a level with removing her bra at the end of a sixteen-hour day or sinking into a bubble bath following a twelve-mile run. The only thing that suppressed her audible rejoicing was her intense desire not to embarrass herself more than she already had with her grand entrance to the lounge earlier.

She'd successfully navigated from her third-floor bedroom to the first-floor lounge, and riding the premature confidence of that minor accomplishment, she'd stepped into the room (late, despite Dottie's warning), instantly lost her footing and toppled into Eric the horse lover (as evidenced by the horse-patterned tie she'd narrowly avoided soaking with his Manhattan). She'd apologized immediately and repeatedly, but he merely stomped away after scowling at her, his downturned mouth disappearing in the thick, dark beard that did little to obscure his weak chin.

"Don't mind him, daffodil." Dottie appeared at her side. "We have Helen to thank for his bad mood. You merely accentuated the negative. Now, let's get you a drink."

Before Maddie had the chance to shift her apologies to her friend and the root cause of her impromptu tumbling act, Carlisle (whose silent approach reinforced Maddie's suspicions that she was some kind of robot-ninja librarian), grabbed her by the arm and steered her toward the drink cart.

"Introduce her to Timothy and then find a safe place for her, maybe over by the windows."

"Of course, Ms. Hunter." Carlisle's grip tightened around her arm.

"Thanks for the assist, Carlisle." Maddie pried the assistant's fingers from her reddened bicep. "But I do know how to walk."

"The evidence suggests otherwise. Besides, damage control is part of my job."

"Lucky me," Maddie grumbled as she wobbled again, and, unbelievably, clutched Carlisle's arm for support.

She didn't release her hold until Carlisle had deposited her in her corner with the dogs, safe from whatever damage she might cause while roaming freely, and close to Timothy, whom Dottie had relieved of his handyman and groundskeeper duties long enough to play the dual role of bartender and butler. That Carlisle hesitated before returning to her more pressing duties both humiliated Maddie further and ushered in a whisper of guilt for her uncharitable thoughts about Dottie's right hand. Not that she was reassessing her entire opinion of the woman, but it was maybe possible that she wasn't entirely unlikeable.

However, the fact that Carlisle had subsequently ignored her was an obstacle to any sort of truce in their unspoken war. True, Maddie resented the help that she'd received (just as begrudgingly as it had been given, no doubt) and had no real desire to repeat the experience. Also true, Maddie's unsure-footed approach to the dinner table had inspired Jason's sister Rebecca to lend her arm (an arm that Maddie absolutely did not notice was attached to a tall, remarkably fit body).

As they made their cautious way to the dining room, Maddie couldn't help but notice the casual elegance of her escort's attire. She looked effortlessly chic in a crimson V-neck blouse and black blazer adorned with a lapel pin. The ensemble fit like it had been made for her, and not even Dottie could argue that Rebecca looked classy (not to mention bewitching) in spite of the fact that she wore slacks. Envy crept in as Maddie regarded Rebecca's dress pants and the admirable way she filled them out.

"Are you going to tell me what's behind me?" Rebecca asked, to Maddie's complete mortification.

"I was just admiring your pants. I mean, the fact that you're in them. I wish I was."

"Did you just say you want to be in my pants?"

"I didn't mean—I just want to get out of this dress." Maddie cringed as soon as the words left her mouth. She didn't need a mirror to know that her face matched the color of Rebecca's shirt. "You don't happen to know of any nearby caves I can hide in, do you?"

"Sorry, I don't." She winked, flustering Maddie further. "But if our positions were reversed, I'd probably say the same thing to you, especially since you look way better in a dress than I ever could."

And now Rebecca had planted herself in the seat next to Maddie's, obviously in case she needed help getting anywhere. Humiliation aside, maybe she had two things to thank Carlisle for.

Much to Dottie's chagrin, surprise guest Helen had seated herself at the head of the table but had thankfully remained quiet. Though she seemed to be scrutinizing and searching for a complaint to lodge, her silence—however short-lived it might be—was a refreshing change from her verbal assaults in the lounge. Though Maddie had spent most of the cocktail hour chatting with Timothy and doling out affection to the never-vigilant Mammon and Archer, she'd also observed Helen from a safe distance. In the short time they'd been gathered in the lounge, Helen had managed to knock back four cocktails while also alienating everyone but Maddie (who she hadn't even acknowledged) and Jason. Her semicivil behavior whenever he was near obviously grated on Dottie, which only seemed to encourage Helen's selective pleasantness.

Florence Saldana, who had the unenviable honor of sitting to Helen's left, fidgeted uncomfortably and checked her silent phone every couple of minutes, each time setting it aside with a sighing groan of disappointment. She hadn't touched her meal, instead concentrating on her wine consumption. Maddie, who couldn't decide if it would be crueler or kinder to inform her of the spotty-at-best cell phone service on the island, had lost track of how many times she'd "topped off" her glass before once again glancing at her disappointing phone.

"Relax, Florence. You're at a party." Helen smiled, almost genuinely, in clear defiance of her mood an hour earlier.

Maddie, tucked away in a corner, flanked by red flocked damask curtains and forgotten as she had been, couldn't help but overhear the less than genial conversation between the two women.

"How do next quarter's projections look?" If it was possible for vocal cords to convey wealth and superiority, Helen's did.

"Good."

"You'll understand if I'm not impressed with such a vague, meaningless response. Where are the numbers?"

"The numbers are in a file on my desk at the office, which I'll have access to on Monday morning," Florence replied.

"When I gave you this promotion, I was under the impression you were up to the task of running a multibillion-dollar corporation."

"We're at a party, Helen."

"I asked for data, not the setting."

"Don't you ever take time off to relax and enjoy yourself?" Florence smiled nervously, and her eyes darted around as if she sought an escape from this conversation.

"I didn't get where I am by taking time off."

"No, but the head start you got from Mom and Dad's money didn't hurt." Castor, looking elegantly carefree in a purple and gray plaid sport coat (adorned with an eye-catching splash of red on his lapel), paused to sneer at his sister. In one hand, he held a half-empty martini glass, while in the other he cradled a surprise guest for the weekend, his dog, Ares, who stared lovingly at Mammon and squirmed to get free.

"If that's all it takes to be successful, why are you such a constant disappointment?"

Florence glanced nervously between the siblings, looking like she'd rather dog paddle back to the mainland than be trapped in their squabble.

"I prefer to think of myself as tedium averse. Keeps me away from dull things like work and my twin sister." He blew a kiss in their direction and continued on his way for a drink.

Helen pivoted on her heels (with a steadiness and grace that Maddie found herself envying). She took two steps before squaring her shoulders and hissing, "If I don't have those numbers in the morning, I'll find someone else to do your job." As Helen sauntered off in the direction of the next unfortunate recipient of her attentions, Maddie was struck with the sudden realization that, for once, Dottie hadn't embellished the truth.

That initial impression had only grown less favorable as Maddie had watched Helen antagonize anyone whose misfortune led them into a conversation with her. Florence had disappeared from the lounge, marking the remainder of the guests as targets for Helen's heightened bad mood. While Maddie doubted that running interference between her guests and Lucifer's sweetheart had been part of Dottie's wooing agenda, the skill with which she rescued Cate, Eric, Castor, and Rebecca was admirable. Judging by Jason's grin as he watched her deft handling of the party crasher from hell (possibly literally), he was equally impressed.

"You hardly touched your soup." Rebecca's low voice in her ear startled her. "Not a fan of broccoli?"

"It's my favorite cruciferous vegetable." She immediately wondered why she ever attempted speech as it so rarely worked out for her. "I guess I was just lost in thought," she said in the direction of the nearly full bowl of broccoli-almond soup that Timothy cleared to make room for the main course.

"Well, don't let my brother see you let food go to waste." She inclined her head in the direction of Jason, whose bowl had been depleted of its contents. Despite his obvious appreciation for dining, he seemed to have no issue with Dottie's preference for fueling herself with booze rather than actual sustenance. Or he simply hadn't noticed, so intent was he on devouring his roast chicken with fennel and carrots. Maddie supposed that a man didn't get to be the size of an alp by holding back at mealtime.

"This is all so delicious. Really, you've outdone yourself." He beamed at Dottie.

"Very convincing, Jason." Helen smiled benevolently, like she was the epitome of kindness and grace. "With more practice like that, you'll have no trouble launching your acting career."

"The wrestling doesn't count?" Castor asked.

"Be nice, Castor dear, or we'll think no one in the Andreas family has any manners." Dottie scowled at Helen as she came to Jason's defense.

Jason, however, was more diplomatic in his response. "It's true that there's a fair amount of showmanship in professional wrestling." Maddie choked on a carrot in her sudden recognition of Jason.

"Are you having a fit?" Dottie hissed.

"More like the preamble to gloating," she murmured before turning her full attention on Jason. "How exciting to be expanding your presence in the industry. You're like a regular *entertainment mogul*." She knew she'd pay for it later, but still she savored every second of Dottie's pained wince.

"Not yet, but maybe someday." Jason flashed a killer smile. Really, he was an incredibly handsome man. "I'd love to be the next Dwayne Johnson."

"You've got my attention. I confess, I love his movies." Cate Bennet, cosmetics magnate and paragon of elegance, was perhaps the last person Maddie expected to profess her adoration of The Rock. "I just love him. I think he's fantastic and so handsome."

"Does my ex-husband know you feel that way?" Helen snarked.

Maddie had almost forgotten that the dark cloud that was Helen hung over the end of the table.

"If you're referring to *my* husband, we don't keep secrets from each other. That's the sort of unhealthy behavior that destroys a relationship."

"Infidelity does the same thing. Ask me how I know."

"As if Randall wasn't halfway out the door when we met."

"And you did everything in your power to encourage him to abandon his family."

"Is that what you think? That's why you're trying to destroy my company."

"Don't be melodramatic, Cate. I'm acquiring your company, bringing it under the Andreas Corp. umbrella. I'm hardly destroying it."

"Same thing if Julieta goes corporate." Dottie sounded appalled, as if the takeover of a cosmetics company was a tragedy on a level with the Shaanxi earthquake. "This can't happen. If you usurp Julieta, it will become the Walmart of cosmetics."

"That's never going to happen. Not if I have anything to say about it," Cate snarled.

"Believe me when I say you don't." Helen's expression was almost feral.

The rest of the party stirred uncomfortably as the two women locked eyes and tension filled the room. Half an eternity passed before Cate rose and excused herself from the table.

"I'm going to call my husband, assuming I can get a cell signal on this damn island."

The stupefied remainder of the party struggled to find some kind of equilibrium following the clash of the business titans, but not even Castor's habitual mischief could deliver a more affable end to their night.

As their fellow diners departed, Carlisle paused by Maddie's side and discreetly pulled a pair of flats from her bag. "I thought perhaps you'd like a fighting chance, but I can hang on to these if you'd prefer." She inclined her head in Rebecca's direction.

Maddie didn't even hesitate to accept this gift from her surprise benefactor. "I don't suppose you have a pair of fuzzy slippers in that Mary Poppins bag?"

Carlisle scowled, not diminishing Maddie's gratitude in the slightest.

CHAPTER THREE

Maddie seldom skipped a day of running, and not even a vacation (planned or otherwise) would change that. So, the next morning, somewhere between sleeping in for her and ungodly early for Dottie, Maddie slipped out for some much-needed exercise and an unofficial tour of the island.

The sprawling, manicured lawn, its vibrant grass rivaling the green of a golf course, sloped down toward the dense woods that stood between her and the shoreline. Maddie was torn between bounding recklessly into the trees to better appreciate the natural beauty of the island and following the stone path encircling the main house and its outlying structures. Swayed (as usual) by her more practical side, she decided to warm up on the less treacherous terrain of the path before satisfying her curiosity in the rough, knurled topography of the woods.

She hadn't made it past the nearby guesthouse before Mammon and Archer came loping up to her. She thought it odd that they were roaming the property alone. Up to that point she'd only seen them alongside their handler, but she supposed that unsupervised strolls could be considered part of their security routine. And with their company, she knew her chances of getting herself lost among the trees or dying of exposure should she succumb to her habitual clumsiness on a remote, secluded area of the island were greatly diminished.

As they moved counterclockwise around the property, passing the guesthouse and the empty stables, she savored the crisp, chilly air that hit her lungs. The trees to her right were alive with the warbling of the various birds who called them home, and occasionally she heard the rustle of leaves, indicating the presence of some mysterious Maine fauna that scurried away before she caught sight of who it might be. It was such a different experience from her standard running exploits in Chicago. There, the soundtrack to her run was more likely to include garbage trucks and poorly functioning mufflers than titmice and chipmunks. And her chances of breathing fresh, ocean-scented air were right up there with Vladimir Putin's hopes for winning a Nobel Peace Prize. At home, bus exhaust fumes were more the order of the day.

But, air quality notwithstanding, she already felt homesick. So much so that after the disastrous dinner and a brief but surprisingly gaffe-free digestif with Rebecca the previous night, she'd tried calling her grandmother with the pretense of making sure Goliath hadn't been dragging her all over the neighborhood, though the prospect of hearing Granny Doyle's voice was a definite perk. But after two dropped calls, Dottie had barged into the room as if she owned it (which, as the sponsor of their weekend adventure, she kind of did) and collapsed melodramatically, even for her, onto the bed.

"Any idea where a girl has to go to get a cell signal?"

"Bangor?"

"You couldn't have rented an island with a cell tower on it?"

"That's the least of my concerns about this particular island." She sat up and smoothed her strawberry-blond locks, which needed precisely zero smoothing. "I can't believe Helen showed up and ruined everything."

"She hasn't ruined anything."

"Bear cub, she can't help but ruin everything. She's a walking natural disaster, a human mushroom cloud."

"She's not that bad," Maddie offered half-heartedly, distracted as she was by maneuvering around her room in vain, in hope of stumbling upon a hidden pocket of cellular connectivity.

"Were you actually enjoying yourself tonight?"

"Not exactly," Maddie admitted. "But I did have my own issues." She looked scornfully at the heels she'd flung into the far corner of her room.

"I blame Helen entirely. She's pure, unadulterated evil. Satan himself fears her."

Maddie had no time to argue before Dottie launched into a ten-minute tirade that bordered on apoplectic. Despite any and all attempts to soothe her friend, Dottie's rage waxed far more than it waned, and though the mansion was a testament to sturdy craftsmanship, not even the most durable walls (or a soundproof booth) could contain Dottie's invective.

"I could strangle her," she growled.

"Calm down, Dottie. It's not that bad. Everyone here knows she invited herself."

"She invited herself in a misguided attempt to woo Jason," Dottie huffed. "As if he'd even consider a tryst with that sea cow."

"Still, you're not to blame."

"How nice. My perfectly planned weekend is a cataclysmic fiasco, but at least it's not my fault. What a relief." As usual, Dottie exaggerated the situation, but out of a strong sense of self-preservation, Maddie refrained from pointing that out. "I should sue her."

"For being insufferable?"

"For breach of contract, spring roll. Try to keep up. I'll have Carlisle call your sister in the morning and get the legal bombardment underway."

"First, as your divorce attorney, June isn't exactly the go-to for legal action pertaining to party remorse. Second, unless Carlisle is as skilled in telepathy as she is at supporting the fashion-compromised, that conversation might have to wait."

She waved her essentially useless cell phone in the air as a reminder of their telecommunications predicament.

"One more grievance for the list."

"Shouldn't you be with Jason?" She changed the subject. "I'd think you would be eager to pin him." Maddie smiled innocently, enjoying this rare opportunity to tease her typically unflappable friend.

"Jason is fetching us a nightcap, allowing me the opportunity to unburden myself to my best friend." A mischievous twinkle in her eye accompanied a lascivious grin. "The pinning will come later."

"Right. You probably have to clothesline him first." Dottie raised an eyebrow in a question. "This would be a lot more fun for me if you knew anything about wrestling."

"I'm sure Jason will help me bone up later."

"Happy to oblige." Jason filled the doorway. He'd removed his suit jacket and tie and rolled up the sleeves of his dress shirt, which seemed ill-equipped for the task of containing his bulging muscles. He wore a fresh-looking bandage on his left forearm, and in one massive hand, he held two glasses of red wine—not Dottie's drink of choice, but there wasn't much in the way of alcohol that she would refuse. He extended his free hand to Dottie and with a killer smile asked, "Shall we?"

Like that, they had departed as abruptly as they'd arrived.

Shaking her head, Maddie returned her attention to the present, and as she and the dogs loped along the path, she wrapped herself in the scenery. Through a less dense patch of trees, she could see the sun glinting off the water, and she heard the crash of waves along the shore near the boathouse. She craned her neck to get a better view of the scenery but instead found herself face-to-face with Rebecca.

"I've been chasing you for half a mile. I didn't know you had it in you." She easily kept pace with Maddie.

"Running?"

"Maintaining your balance."

"Blame the sensible shoes."

"I kind of miss the heels." She glanced down at Maddie's feet and didn't bother to hide her grin as her eyes traveled back up to Maddie's face. "But you look good like this too."

Maddie kept her face studiously forward, hoping that her blush would be interpreted as red-faced exertion. Not that that would be much better. By all appearances, Rebecca was a fitness junkie. Maybe that was a byproduct of having a professionally fit sibling.

"Were you out for a run?" Maddie tried to sound casual, though her exertion pretty much prevented anything approaching carefree ease in conversation.

"I was in the guesthouse with Jason."

"The mansion wasn't big enough for you?" Maddie deftly avoided Archer, who crossed her path carrying a stick so large it may have qualified as a log.

"There's a home gym there," she explained. "Jason works out every day, and he has a habit of recruiting those nearest and dearest. I knew the risks when I agreed to this vacation."

"Why didn't he join you on your run?"

"He doesn't have the, ah, appreciation for cardio that I do. I find it irresistible at times."

"Well, what's not to love with all the heavy breathing and working up a sweat?"

Thankfully Maddie's face was red before she uttered that sentence. Still, she increased her speed despite the near impossibility of outrunning her mortification, especially since her new running buddy easily kept up with her. As usual, she was out of her depths. "Looks like a storm is coming." She hitched her chin in the direction of a particularly angry cloud in an otherwise blue sky. Dottie would not be pleased with Mother Nature's intrusion on her plans. She'd probably blame Helen.

"It's just one cloud. I'm sure it will blow over." Rebecca ran ahead of her and turned back in a challenge. "How much farther were you going?"

"I was thinking of heading to the teahouse, mostly so I can try to figure out what a teahouse is." She ignored the nervous flutter in her stomach. "Care to join me?"

"Wouldn't you rather head to the dock and enjoy the scenery? I'll race you."

Maddie's competitive side flared to the surface, but her circumspection wasn't yet ready to give up control. "What about the storm?"

"What storm? This will pass before lunchtime."

She didn't have the same confidence, but rather than argue, she took off in the direction of the finish line.

When they entered the mansion almost an hour later, they discovered a house in turmoil, at least of a mild variety. Carlisle, having reverted to fashion form in slacks and her standard sweater set, bustled into the lounge where most of the guests had gathered. Aside from Florence, who wrung her hands anxiously, their postures indicated varying degrees of disinterest or hangover.

"Still no sign of her, Ms. Hunter, but we haven't checked all of the rooms yet."

"Thank you, Carlisle. Let me know when she's found." Dottie eyed the drink cart but apparently thought better of a cocktail before noon. "I should have expected something like this."

"What's going on?" Forgetting about her disheveled state and Dottie's aversion to perspiration, Maddie rushed to her friend's side.

"Helen might be missing."

"You're not sure?"

"No one has seen her since she derailed our evening."

"Don't ask me why we're so eager to change that," Cate added. Looking effortlessly elegant in gray slacks and a cream-colored blouse, she perched delicately on the edge of Helen's flocked electric-blue loveseat, the plenitude of allegedly decorative, oversize gold satin pillows encroaching on her space. Apparently having exhausted the limits of her concern for Helen's whereabouts, she turned her attention back to her coffee.

"I'm as eager to bring her back into the circle as I am to have an entirely polyester wardrobe," Dottie said. "But her chances of a sneak attack are greater if we don't know where she is."

"Are we sure she isn't just sleeping it off?" Rebecca asked. "She did drink a lot last night."

"Her room is empty, and the maid said that the bed hadn't been slept in. Unless she made her own bed, but it seems like an odd time for her to suddenly become domestic."

"You don't think she knows how to make a bed? That's pretty basic on the housekeeping scale," Maddie said.

"My sister's motto is never do for yourself what you can pay someone a subsistence wage to do for you." Castor stifled a yawn, his concern about his twin's well-being clear.

"How charming," Dottie remarked.

Just then, a horrified shriek pierced the air, and Maddie's next question died on her lips.

CHAPTER FOUR

"What now?" Dottie cried.

"Nothing good, I'm guessing." Maddie rushed to the door and popped her head into the hallway, simultaneously hoping to find the cause of the scream and to remain clueless.

"Wonderful. What this fiasco of a weekend needed was another sampling of nothing good." Dottie's scowl somehow managed to look at least equal parts elegant and displeased. "Must you seek out danger wherever you go, Calamity Jane? Get away from that door and hide like a sensible person."

"Aren't you at all curious about who screamed and why?"

"What's life without a little mystery?"

"It could be Helen," Carlisle suggested, earning a stern glare from her employer. Nevertheless, she joined Maddie in the doorway, ready to take on the unknown.

"We should go help," Rebecca said and joined the swelling crowd at the door.

"Define *we*." Castor's interest was pretty evenly divided between his missing and possibly imperiled sister, his dog (who gazed across the room longingly at Mammon) and his silk scarf, the knot of which was apparently not sitting properly.

"It definitely includes me," Jason announced in his voiceover-perfect baritone. The only thing missing from his consummate heroism was the flexing of his boulder-size biceps.

"Naturally you'll want to include me. I'm invaluable in an emergency," Dottie, apparently valuing time with Jason over her own discomfort, overstated the likelihood of her contribution.

Eric sidled up to Rebecca, who spared a moment to roll her eyes. "We'll all go," he said.

"Have fun." Cate, her expression somewhere between indifferent and indignant, didn't budge from the loveseat.

Jason seemed bewildered by Cate's indifference. "You aren't coming?"

"Join the imminent peril brigade for a woman who's more likely to kick a puppy than have even one kind thought about another human being ever? I'll pass."

"What if this is a clever ruse to get you alone?" Dottie asked.

"To what end?"

"You'll have to ask the psychopath who caused all the screaming."

Shuddering at the dramatic (and highly unlikely) scenario Dottie proposed, Cate grimaced but rose to join the group, moving as near to Jason's imposing figure as possible.

"How did this mysterious psychopath get to the private island that the rest of us had to access by helicopter?" Maddie whispered to Dottie. "It's probably just a mouse."

"As if this weekend isn't cursed enough."

Just then, another scream rang out, effectively ending the discussion. Not entirely certain where the screeching had emanated from, they ran toward the back of the house, some at a more noticeably brisk pace than others. Leading the pack with Maddie were Jason, Rebecca, and a surprisingly fleet-footed Carlisle, whose librarian-chic attire belied the sprinter within.

They scurried past the ballroom, the dining room, the billiard room, two bathrooms and the conservatory as they hunted for the source of the commotion. At several points along their infinite journey, one of them (usually Eric) poked their head in the door in search of the hubbub, but each time the room turned up empty.

"Assuming Helen and the person screaming aren't one and the same, this will make our renewed search for her all the faster," Carlisle offered brightly after yet another of Eric's fruitless forays from the hallway that never ended.

"Is this really the time to rhapsodize on the benefits of multitasking?" Dottie snapped.

"There's never a wrong time to appreciate multitasking."

Maddie, who had hoped that an embarrassing outing in heels would be the nadir of her weekend adventure with Dottie, had the sinking feeling that she was about to relive one of the more gruesome experiences of her life. Of course, she had no way of knowing what they would find (assuming they ever found anything in this paean to architectural excess), but she doubted it was anything as innocent as a rodent—a visceral scream like that came from a place of terror, not squeamishness. Though she hoped she was overreacting, she feared that this weekend was about to take a very bad turn, one that would make her long for the simplicity of footwear-based humiliation.

"Must we sprint?" Dottie huffed. "These shoes were not made for running."

"Neither was my hangover," Florence groaned. She pressed one hand to her forehead while the other clutched her side. She looked dangerously close to vomiting. "Who extended the hallway?"

"Helen," Castor hissed, "just to make us suffer." He had been bringing up the rear with Florence, but the more nauseous she appeared, the more he increased the gap between them.

An eternity later, breathless, frenzied, and on the verge of surrender, they reached the kitchen, its gleaming marble counters overflowing with ingredients for what should have been an extravagant breakfast. In her cursory glance, Maddie saw dozens of eggs, cream, bread, three different cheeses, the requisite rasher of bacon and for those nursing a sweet tooth, a wealth of maple syrup, the kind that didn't come in a woman-shaped bottle. She imagined it would be a delight for the senses and sure to set her workout regimen back at least a week—or it would have if the chef was anywhere in the vicinity. That the cook was the only thing absent from the fully stocked kitchen was yet another cause for alarm.

"I can't believe it, but we're running out of house to search," Rebecca said.

Carlisle pointed a finger in the air. "You're forgetting the upper stories." Among her many talents, she could always be counted on to inject a dose of discouraging reality.

"At least the wine cellar is locked, so we know we won't have to search there," Cate offered optimistically.

"You were saying?" Florence pointed to the wine cellar door, which stood wide open, in clear defiance of Helen's restrictions.

"I'll kill her if she's hiding out in her exclusive wine cellar while we're wasting time hunting for her." Dottie's snarl was surprisingly unrefined.

"We can't go down there," Castor said, scowling at Mammon, who assertively sniffed at the small dog in his arms.

"We have to," Rebecca insisted.

"And risk making Helen even more unpleasant? No, thank you," Cate added.

"Obviously something happened down there. It's not like Helen would have left the door open to tempt us into the one place she forbade us from entering."

"You clearly don't know my sister." He clutched Ares closer to him and tried evading Mammon's persistent interest in the little dog.

"We have to know what happened, and we can't find that out standing around up here." Maddie swallowed hard, already regretting what she was about to say. "I'll go. Helen doesn't seem to know I exist, so maybe I'll be safe."

"Absolutely not, larkspur. I won't have you rushing into danger like that."

"Do you have a better idea?"

"I'll go with her," Rebecca volunteered. "She'll be safe."

"I'm sure you make a fine bodyguard, lady Jason, but Matilda attracts danger like picnics attract ants. I wouldn't trust the National Guard to keep her safe."

Maddie opened her mouth to object but thought better of it. Dottie had a point.

"Perhaps we should all go together," Carlisle suggested. "Safety in numbers, after all."

"Tell that to the people at Jonestown," Dottie countered.

Frustration mounting, Maddie snapped, "We should definitely do more than stand around debating our next move."

"Fine, lava cake, let's all put ourselves at risk."

Despite being the one who argued the case for exploring the forbidden realms of the wine cellar, Maddie didn't charge down the stairs once she got the go-ahead. Rather, she crept forward, no member of her eclectic backup rushing her in the slightest.

"Is this Brazilian mahogany?" Eric marveled, eyeing the handrail. "It's exquisite."

"For a room that no one but my sister gets to appreciate. It's a waste."

"Also a little beside the point," Maddie grumbled, her dread mounting with every step closer to the bottom of the staircase. She felt oddly worse once she took in the terrifying scene in the wine cellar.

There in the dead center of the stone floor lay Helen, surrounded by her precious wine collection. Beside her, unconscious but still breathing, was the terrified maid, and Chef Barbara hovered over them both, busily fanning the young woman with her apron.

"Is she dead?" Florence gasped.

"I think she just passed out from the shock," Jason said. "See, she's moving."

"I meant Helen."

"Well, I highly doubt she opted to sleep in the wine cellar, no matter how nicely appointed she thinks it is." Dottie spared a moment to admire the vintages on display.

"Was it a heart attack?" Eric asked.

"Wouldn't that require a heart?" Castor answered.

"What do we do now?" Cate's voice broke, and she turned away from the scene on the floor.

"We need to call the police," Carlisle said.

"How? Our cell phones are essentially useless," Maddie reminded her.

"Surely Helen has a landline," Florence said. "How could she relax if she couldn't reach out and torment someone?"

"She wanted this to be her sanctuary from her life as taskmaster and business overlord," Castor explained with an almost sorrowful shake of the head. "Which is why she rarely spent any time here."

"Well then, we need to go to the mainland and get the police to come here." Carlisle took three efficient steps toward the stairs.

"All of us?" Florence seemed more dismayed by this prospect than by the corpse splayed on the stone floor.

"Shouldn't someone stay with…the body?" Jason asked.

"Who gets stuck with that job?" Eric seemed genuinely terrified that it would be him.

As they argued over corpse-sitting duties, Maddie saw that Archer had abandoned his stick in favor of chewing on Helen's shoe (which, thankfully, lay empty beside her). In spite of every instinct she had urging her in the opposite direction, she moved closer to the body. She knelt to discreetly put an end to his somewhat morbid snacking, and that's when she noticed that the dead woman's eyes—so eerily fixed on the ceiling—were bloodshot. Looking closer, she saw a splotchy rash on Helen's face. In every mystery, cop, and forensic show Maddie had ever watched, a rash like that pointed to strangulation. Though it was entirely possible that Helen was allergic to the wine she'd been enjoying or something else on the island and that Maddie was simply the victim of an overactive imagination, that didn't explain the bruising and scratches on her neck, did it?

Likewise, the bloodshot eyes could just as easily indicate choking as strangulation, and if Helen had choked while all alone in her wine cellar as she had commanded, the chances of anyone coming to her rescue with the Heimlich maneuver were nonexistent. Would she have clawed at her own throat to try to save herself? Possibly. She might even have done so with such force that she'd torn her own blouse, sending buttons flying. So maybe it had been an unfortunate but entirely natural death. But it didn't seem likely. So no, Maddie didn't have the credentials to state with certainty that this was a murder, but there was no doubt in her mind that someone on this island had killed Helen.

She rose to address the still bickering crowd. "More importantly how do we decide who leaves the island?"

"What do you mean?" Castor asked.

"Someone here killed her."

"How can you possibly know that?" Eric asked. "Maybe she choked on a chicken bone."

"Do you see any chicken around here?"

"We had chicken for dinner."

"Not with bones in it." Chef Barbara crossed her arms and scowled.

"Do you honestly believe that she tore her own blouse or bruised her own neck?"

"I wouldn't put anything past my sister, especially if it will ruin someone else's good time."

"Implausible theories aside," Maddie steered the conversation back on course, "what if we send the murderer to get the police and never see them again?"

"Wouldn't that be a dead giveaway? Pardon the pun."

"Yes, but with a two-day head start, the killer could be anywhere by the time the rest of us leave the island."

"What are the chances that the person we send happens to be the killer?" Cate asked.

Florence flapped her hands near her face and groaned. "But if we don't, that leaves the rest of us here with a murderer."

"What are our other options?" Rebecca asked. "Play *Weekend at Bernie's* until the helicopter comes back on Monday?"

"What about the butler?" Jason asked.

"Good thinking." Dottie was a thousand times more enthusiastic than was appropriate in the moment. "He makes an exceptional martini."

"I meant that we could send him for the police."

"Of course. You're absolutely right. Carlisle, fetch Timothy, would you?"

"He's missing, ma'am," the maid, now upright but still dangerously pale, spoke softly.

"What do you mean 'ma'am'?" Dottie said.

"Not the point, Dottie," Maddie hissed. "What do you mean he's missing?"

"He was supposed to take care of breakfast service, but he never showed. But since Mr. Van Dam and his sister were the only people who wanted breakfast"—she smiled shyly at Jason—"it didn't seem to matter."

"I haven't seen him either," the chef offered. "Not since last night. He said he had an appointment with the lady of the house so he would take care of locking everything up and would see me in the morning, but so far nothing."

"What are the chances that he's sleeping in?" Maddie asked.

"I have a very bad feeling about this," Florence moaned.

"You think he killed Helen and fled the scene." Dottie put forth a less believable theory than Maddie's optimistic hope that Timothy had discovered his slacker side.

"I'd call that the best-case scenario," Maddie sighed, fearing that whoever killed Helen also murdered Timothy.

"Oh my god," Castor gasped, a wicked gleam in his eye, "are you saying that the butler did it?"

"So now what do we do?" Cate asked testily, her patience for Castor's morbid humor wearing thin.

"Maddie can investigate," Dottie stated.

"I can what?"

"You've done it before."

"I've also broken a bone before. I'm not really looking to repeat the experience."

"Tartlet, in case you haven't noticed, we're fresh out of options. The police aren't going to magically appear, and whoever did this is still among us until the helicopter returns on Monday morning to deliver us from this cursed island. I'd rather not sit around waiting to be picked off by a deranged killer."

"I think maybe that's a bit of a leap," Maddie argued. "Just because someone killed Helen—"

"And possibly the butler," Carlisle offered helpfully.

"That doesn't mean they're going to try to kill the rest of us."

"And you really feel comfortable taking that chance?"

She glanced at the room full of virtual strangers, none of whom she had any reason to trust and most of whom had genuine reason to want Helen dead.

"Here we go again," she muttered.

CHAPTER FIVE

"Where do we start, dumpling?"

"How about by taking a giant step back." Castor pushed himself to the front of the small crowd gathered around his sister's body. After a brief glance at Helen, he retreated one step and focused his attention on Dottie. "Don't we get a say in this?"

"What would you like to say?"

"That this is a serious matter, one that requires more expertise than can be expected from a professional pooper scooper."

"Kind of judgmental for a man whose résumé consists of squandering his inheritance and dodging his bookie."

"Snobbery aside, he's not the only one who doesn't like this idea." Cate leaned against the wall farthest from Helen's body and kept her gaze resolutely at eye level.

"What's not to like about allowing a seasoned detective to root out the killer among us?"

"Let's start with her obvious loyalty to you," Castor said.

"Not a problem since I did nothing wrong."

"I can say the same, but your *seasoned* detective isn't likely to take my word on that."

"And how do we really know that Helen was murdered?" Eric spoke up, his voice tremulous. "Are we just supposed to believe your friend? She's not exactly a medical examiner, is she?"

"Not even close," Carlisle blurted, earning a glare from Maddie. "But among us, I believe she's the most experienced with unnatural death."

"How can you be sure this wasn't natural?" Cate gestured to Helen's body, still not bothering to look at it, and Maddie wondered if she was seeing something that wasn't there.

She again looked at Helen's supine form, instantly regretting it. Just what cried out murder rather than an accidental or a natural death? Despite every ounce of her begging her not to, she studied the woman on the floor, cataloguing the clues to support her claims.

"You mean aside from the bloodshot eyes, bruised neck, torn shirt and the red marks all over her face?" Maddie snapped. "Let's call it a hunch. Look, I hope I'm wrong," she said to Eric, "but what if I'm right? Do you really want to take that chance? Do you want to spend the rest of the weekend wondering if you're enjoying canapes with a killer?"

Eric glanced nervously around the room, whether in fear of a killer or of being caught, Maddie couldn't tell. "I suppose you're right. None of us will relax until we know what happened."

"Except the killer," Jason said. "I doubt he's worried about being murdered."

"No, but he should be worried about being caught." Dottie's vote of confidence provided little relief for Maddie. She had no idea how she was supposed to discover Helen's killer among a pool of suspects whose overwhelming reluctance would almost certainly translate into underwhelming cooperation. "Matilda has captured not one but two murderers in the past year, with considerable assistance from me, of course." She flipped her hair as nimbly as she stretched the truth. "So tell us, petite Poirot, what's our next move?"

"I think the first thing we need to do is find Timothy."

"How will that help?" Cate asked disdainfully.

"You mean aside from his mastery of the cocktail shaker?" Dottie asked.

Maddie suppressed an eye roll at her friend's relentless pursuit of intoxication.

"I just don't see why we have to go tromping all over the island on the chance that the butler is missing," Cate continued. "He might simply be taking a stroll. Besides which, these are designer shoes."

"Of course they are," Rebecca muttered.

"Timothy is a consummate professional, not likely to take a walkabout at the apex of his responsibilities."

"Didn't you hire him from a rental service in Portland?" Cate snapped.

"That was the maid. And her ratings are stellar," Dottie huffed.

"The point"—Maddie tried to return their focus to the matter at hand—"is that we have reason to believe that Timothy is missing, and either he knows something and is hiding, or he knew something and is now dead."

"Or," Florence spoke up, "he finally had enough of Helen, realized that no paycheck was worth the abuse and decided to take his chances swimming back to civilization."

"She speaks from experience," Cate said.

"But why wouldn't he just take a boat?" Eric's question reinforced the notion that both sarcasm and hyperbole were lost on him.

"Because my sister never learned to share, so she keeps the key to the boathouse locked away. Either way, we'll need a new bartender." Castor aligned himself with the small but powerful survival-by-inebriation camp.

"Is that really what we should be worried about?" Jason frowned his disapproval, and Maddie couldn't help but notice that even his facial muscles were toned.

"Of course not, love, especially since Maddie is a mixologist par excellence."

"Won't she be too busy solving Helen's murder to make martinis?" Cate asked.

"I prefer a good Manhattan." Eric glanced at Maddie expectantly.

"She'll multitask," Dottie explained wryly.

"Apparently, I'm going to be busy, so we need to work fast. That means we should split up."

"Split up how?" Florence objected, and Maddie wondered if she would have to debate every move she made. If she was going to have to investigate by committee, she had no hope of finding the killer before the weekend was over. "I don't want to go off into the wilderness with whoever could do that to Helen."

"That's a good point," Eric chimed in. "It would be safer if we all stick together."

"Safer but slower," Rebecca said.

"I still like my plan of hiding in our rooms until this weekend is over." Cate pouted.

"Because cold-blooded killers seldom know how to open doors," Dottie said.

"Sarcasm accomplishes nothing, Gwendolyn. It also causes wrinkles." Cate arched an eyebrow and pointed a manicured finger at Dottie, who shuddered in appropriate horror.

"Please. Anyone could do that to Helen. I just met her yesterday, and I could do that to her." The assembled group gaped at Rebecca. "I didn't," she quickly added.

"Groups of three." Carlisle returned their discussion to the point. "It's the safest and most efficient option we have now."

"And with the storm that's heading our way, I think we need to be quick about this." A rumble of thunder validated Maddie's concerns.

"How exactly will a spring shower impact our hunt for the butler?" Castor asked. "Is he likely to dissolve?"

"I'm just thinking of Cate's shoes."

"Speaking of showers, Matilda," Dottie whispered, "you could stand to freshen up."

"How foolish of me not to plan my post-run bathing around the possibility of a murder."

"We should get started," Carlisle said, again nudging them back in the direction of productivity.

"How do we pick the groups?" Castor asked. "No offense to Eric, but if I'm going to confront death, I'd rather be with someone butch like Becky over there."

"Call me Becky again, and you won't live long enough to find out who killed your sister."

"Exactly the kind of muscle I want at my side when on the hunt for a truant butler."

"We could draw straws," Maddie suggested. The last thing she wanted was to relive junior high gym class, where she'd been preordained to be the last person picked for every team, no matter the sport. "Do we have straws?"

"I've got some bamboo skewers upstairs," Chef Barbara answered. "Would that work?"

"Eco-friendly and not in the same room as the corpse? That's what I call a win-win." Eric didn't wait for further discussion before trotting up the stairs and escaping the grim confines of the wine cellar.

A short while later, after the grumbling and shuffling about the kitchen subsided, they stood in their respective groups, trying to decide how best to conduct their search. Maddie took small comfort in the knowledge that not one of them seemed pleased with the results of their randomly generated groups.

After being lumped with Florence and Carlisle, Castor complained at length about getting stuck with the pasty librarian and the skittish lesbian, arriving at a slightly more favorable conclusion only after a particularly dour glare from Carlisle.

"Still, it's better than Eric the Chickenhearted."

"Only for you." Carlisle began marshalling Castor and Florence out the door. "We'll start in the teahouse."

"We'll check the stables," Eric announced, eliciting a disapproving groan from Dottie. She eschewed all things rustic, and Maddie suspected she would have been far more content searching the drink cart for her missing butler.

"Must we?"

"I'm the best person for the job. I'll know if anything is off."

"Unless he's disguised himself as oats, I don't think we'll be needing your expertise," Rebecca said, failing to mask her irritation.

"Well, maybe you'll have use for some of my other passions." He winked, and everyone else in the room shuddered in unison.

"Let's just get this over with." Dottie led her group out the door, followed shortly by Maddie, Cate, and Jason on their way to the guesthouse.

And that's how she'd ended up on the threshold of the guesthouse, sandwiched between the picture of male virility and the empress of artificial beauty. The building—easily the size of her own home—loomed over them, and Maddie felt marginally better that she wasn't the only one reluctant to enter.

She wished that she'd ended up with Dottie in her group. Not that she minded working with her own personal colossus (assuming he wasn't the killer), but she would have preferred Dottie's quest for alcohol to Cate's sullen disinterest. Neither was exactly productive, but at least she knew how to work with the former. Though, as far as the investigation was concerned, Maddie supposed it was better that they'd been separated by the whims of the bamboo skewer. She hoped they could compare notes later, assuming Dottie recovered from her time in the stables and that the panel of suspects granted them time alone.

"What kind of person needs a guesthouse when they have a thirteen-bedroom mansion at their disposal?" She couldn't imagine entertaining that many people at once.

"Someone with a lot of friends?" Jason suggested.

"That excludes Helen." Cate looked to Jason and hitched her chin at the door.

Taking the cue, Jason squared his shoulders, opened the door and called out, "Hello?"

Maddie couldn't decide if she was more relieved or disappointed that the only answer was a clap of thunder issuing another warning of the impending storm.

Just like the mansion they were staying in, this space was questionably decorated. The marble floor of the foyer shimmered in the light from a grandiose crystal chandelier. The foyer led to a sweeping stairway, and just to the right was a small study (containing an oversize oil portrait of Helen, a woman whose features were more suited to abstract painting than realism) and a powder room so ostentatious it put Versailles to shame. To the left there was a small kitchen and dining room—small only in comparison to the main house. Matilda's own home would seem like a linen closet in comparison.

Atrocious décor notwithstanding, the architecture itself commanded attention. If not for the dark cloud of a possible double homicide hanging over her head, Maddie would have liked to examine the space, with its pristine woodwork and vaulted ceilings. She stood in the foyer for a moment, admiring the ornate plasterwork on the ceiling when Cate broke in on her thoughts.

"We're looking for the butler, not Spider-Man. I doubt he's up there."

"Right." Maddie laughed uncomfortably, wishing (not for the first time) that she'd stuck to her original reclusive agenda for the weekend.

"So, this is something you do regularly?" Jason glanced back as he led them into the kitchen.

"Not if I can help it." Maddie scanned the room, seeing no signs of the butler or any activity in the last several weeks.

"Then why are you so eager to play detective now?" Cate, attention fully focused on her manicured fingernails, didn't even pretend to look for Timothy.

"Believe me, I'd rather devote my attention to celebrating my friend, but it seems a bit foolish to ignore the situation in favor of a party, don't you think?"

For an answer, Cate shrugged and half-heartedly glanced in a cabinet, as if they'd be likely to find the six-foot-something Timothy tucked away like canned beans.

"Is there a reason you don't want me to investigate?"

"Other than your lack of qualifications? None at all." She grimaced and opened a drawer. Apparently, she'd decided that Timothy had fallen victim to a shrinking ray. Or she had good reason to believe that a search of the guesthouse's kitchen was a waste of time.

"Is that one of your moves?" Jason asked.

"My moves?"

"For investigations. Do you trick people into revealing the truth without knowing that's what they're doing? Like through their answers to other questions?"

Cate blanched at the suggestion, and Maddie almost regretted putting her at ease. "I'm nowhere near that clever."

"And now you've thrown us off with self-deprecation. I love this." He pumped his fist in the air before leading them into the dining room, with its total lack of hiding places for a butler or a body.

"I promise I'm not engaged in any kind of subterfuge." But Maddie wasn't sure she could say the same for Cate, who made an exaggerated show of looking beneath the dining room table for a body that would have been obscured by nothing.

"No butler there." She dusted off her hands and turned her attention to the Waterford cruet on the sideboard. Perhaps she believed Timothy was a genie that she could call forth from his glass prison. Or she was simply bored and looking for other amusements.

"Why are you so interested in my investigation techniques?" Even for someone as enthusiastic as Jason, he was far too curious about Maddie's search for the killer.

"I can't really talk about it because the deal hasn't been finalized, but I'm preparing for my first big dramatic role. It's a modern retelling of Sherlock Holmes."

Another one? Maddie thought as both she and Cate looked him up and down quizzically. How on earth could this hulking boulder of a human be considered for any interpretation of Holmes? She wasn't sure she wanted to know the thought process that went into that casting decision.

She asked the second most pressing question in her mind. "Is this the movie Helen was investing in?"

"It is. She was looking forward to her debut as a producer."

"So is the movie in danger now that she's, um, no longer participating?"

"It's probably better off. She was being kind of demanding about some of the casting decisions."

"Such as?"

"She thought I'd make a better henchman for the villain. It's not a speaking part."

Just then a breathless Carlisle burst into the room, halting their search and their conversation. "We found him," she gasped. "We found Timothy."

CHAPTER SIX

They raced across the grounds to the teahouse (Cate's precious shoes be damned). As they ran, dark clouds filled the sky, the wind furiously whipped Maddie's ponytail about her head, and the impending storm (the one no one listened to her about) urged them toward the shelter of the teahouse. They were stopped at the door by Castor, who had apparently adopted the role of bouncer. Not even the looming tempest impacted his resolve.

"Trust me, you don't want to go in there." He gently petted Ares, who trembled in his arms.

"There's a storm of biblical proportions headed our way, so no matter what's in there, I'll take it over braving a nor'easter in just my running clothes."

Mammon whined and leaned against Maddie's legs while Archer unleashed a plaintive howl. Maddie wondered if the dogs were nervous about the storm or if something else was causing their anxiety.

"Really, man. Just let us in." Jason towered over Castor, but the smaller man didn't relent. "How bad could it be?"

"It's gruesome."

"What is it? An honest day's work?"

"Now, now, Catie. Helen's death doesn't mean you have to fill the relentless bitch void."

"My calf-hair pumps have grass stains because we rushed to get here." She gestured to her defiled footwear. "Don't make me add blood stains to the collection of fashion crosses that I currently bear."

"This accomplishes nothing." Carlisle's admonishment did little to squelch their argument.

"Had I known we'd be barred from entering once we arrived, I wouldn't have endangered the Manolos."

"Poor girl. My deepest condolences on such a tragic loss, but we still have to wait for everyone to get here." Castor's tone oozed smarm.

"Why? Our crack detective is here." Cate sneered in Maddie's direction. "What more could we need?" She tried pushing past him.

"You don't really want to blow the big reveal, do you?"

"Can you tell us anything?" Maddie asked, both to put an end to their bickering and because she wanted some idea of what she was about to walk into.

"Only that this was no *ax*-ident."

Lightning flashed nearby followed by the rumble of thunder as the storm approached, but Castor's cryptic answer seemed more foreboding than whatever Mother Nature had in store. She was about to ask for an explanation when the remainder of the group approached.

"We discovered nothing in the stables except that I was right to avoid them." Dottie frowned at Eric's back. "What awaits us in the teahouse?"

"He's dead, isn't he?" Rebecca called from the walkway, a still fawning Eric encroaching on her personal space.

"Spoken like the guilty party, Becky."

She glared at Castor. "If he isn't dead, we would all be back at the main house instead of meeting here."

"Smart and athletic," Dottie whispered to Maddie. "You should snap her up, toots."

"I'll take it under advisement."

"Well, if she's half the paramour her brother is—"

In a desperate attempt to prevent any details of Jason's carnal capabilities, Maddie blurted, "What is a teahouse anyway?"

"Apparently the ideal place to kill the butler." Castor opened the door and stepped aside. "See for yourselves."

The group filtered in, but Maddie hesitated on the threshold. Logically she knew that Rebecca was right—Timothy was dead, most likely murdered. But until she saw him, she could remain in happy denial that she was vacationing with a killer. Once she went inside and saw whatever had flustered the normally unflappable Carlisle, there was no going back.

"Nothing wrong with easing into it," she muttered as she focused on the space itself.

Though it was undeniably posh, there was nothing specifically tea-related about the octagonal sitting room. With its pristine white walls, soaring ceilings with ornate plaster molding, generous floorplan and large, arched windows, it felt airy and open, like the perfect place to gather for drinks or dessert. The large fireplace along the west wall meant that, even in the chill of winter, this was an ideal spot for entertaining. A cozy seating area with an overstuffed maroon leather couch and chairs on a blue Persian rug invited guests to gather for conversation or to admire the breathtaking view of the shoreline. If not for the task at hand, she might have been tempted to lounge in one of the equally bloated chairs and watch the storm brew outside.

But as the not-so-subtle clearing of Dottie's throat reminded her, they weren't here for the scenery. Reluctantly, she tore her gaze from the windows and continued her perusal of the space. The wall opposite the fireplace boasted a pair of John Singer Sargent portraits. Magnificent as they were, they were obviously not intended as the artistic showpieces. That honor was apparently meant for the three separate portraits of Helen, painted in the image of Sargent's work and accented with gilded frames. The work was striking but unsettling, considering their subject's recent demise. No matter where Maddie looked, every touch seemed designed to highlight a borderline-excessive display of wealth.

Turning to her left, she spotted a grand piano in the corner farthest from her. The lid was propped open, and the music rack held sheet music, as if a performance were imminent. She spied an inconspicuous hall near the piano and wondered where it led, but for now her attention remained on the gentleman seated at the piano. Adding to the illusion of an impending concert, Timothy, still in his tuxedo from the night before, sat on the piano bench. If not for the fact that he slumped forward on the keys, an ax in his back and blood pooling on the otherwise unblemished flagstone floor beneath him, it would have been just one more ostentatious touch to an already overblown room.

"Shouldn't you go look at the body? Won't that make it easier to investigate?" Jason's question crashed in on her thoughts. Brutal death apparently did nothing to quell his enthusiasm.

"Easier but not more pleasant."

If she was going to solve this murder, she would need more than the hazy details evident from her more palatable distance from the corpse. Despite an overwhelming desire to run away, she crept closer, all eyes on her, and confronted the irrefutable evidence that there was, in fact, a murderer among them.

She realized then that she had been hoping for almost any outcome other than this. Not only because she didn't relish the thought of investigating another murder, but also because she liked Timothy, or what she knew of him. In the brief time she'd spent talking to him when she'd been relegated to the corner during the cocktail hour, she'd learned that he was a recent widower and had two grown children. She'd honestly looked forward to being stuck in the corner with him again that evening. Instead, she would be trying to find out who killed him.

Within thirty seconds of closer proximity, she could tell that the killer had struck Timothy more than once, though she had no way of knowing exactly how many times or if any blows after the first had been necessary. Whoever had wielded the ax had been viciously thorough, but why such brutality? Swallowing her revulsion, she turned away from his injuries to consider the fuller picture and hopefully find some clues.

His right cheek rested against the sheet music and his lifeless stare was fixed on his left arm, outstretched across the keys. It was almost as if his killer had come upon him midsong and brought a horrific end to the performance. But that seemed preposterous. For one thing, what was Timothy doing in the teahouse while everyone was sleeping? To her knowledge, none of Dottie's party plans involved the teahouse. She would double-check, but for all its architectural assets, the teahouse lacked the grandeur Dottie sought in a venue. But even if Timothy had a legitimate reason for being there, why would he have been sitting at the piano? Of all the late-night behaviors a person could engage in, midnight piano practice seemed bizarre and unlikely.

And then there was the blood—there should have been more. Not that the pool on the floor was in any way unimpressive, but wouldn't the ceiling and surrounding walls show some indication of the killer's thoroughness? But not a cobweb or speck of dust marred their blindingly white surfaces, let alone blood spatter.

The floor, however, told a different story. Having no real idea what, if anything, she should be looking for, she crouched beside Timothy to get a closer look. His feet rested on the pedals, which meant that his shoes (the toes thoroughly scuffed and daubed with blood but otherwise in pristine condition) had been spared further damage from the blood pooling below him, though Maddie supposed that didn't matter now.

From that vantage point, she could see a trail of blood, the drops smeared as if something (or more likely, someone) had been dragged through them, leading down the hallway. If she followed the trail, she might find some answers, like where Timothy had been murdered because she was certain it hadn't been here. That was a long way from understanding who killed him or why, but she had to start somewhere.

She rose to explore her only lead and came face to strapping chest with Jason.

"Find anything good?" he asked.

"I'm not sure yet." She turned back to the clue but was interrupted again.

"Don't keep us in suspense, leaflet. What's the verdict?" Dottie called from her sheltered position on the other side of the room.

She groaned inwardly, knowing that her focus would never return to the literal trail the killer had left until she gave Dottie some information. "It's safe to say this death wasn't natural."

"Why would anyone kill the butler?" Florence sank into one of the chairs and released a weary breath.

"Perhaps he struck the wrong chord with someone." Castor looked around the room, finding no appreciative audience for his humor. "Too soon?"

"I'm not sure why he was killed, but I'm betting whoever's responsible for this, murdered Helen as well." All eyes were on her, expecting answers or some kind of explanation, but she had none.

"That poor man," Cate gasped. She collapsed onto the couch and buried her face in her hands.

"How can you be traumatized by the death of a man you didn't care enough about to want to search for?" Rebecca snapped.

"Well, it's my first bloodied corpse, so pardon me for not acting like a cyborg."

"Let's not argue." Dottie stepped between the two, who were getting dangerously close to one another. "This day has been stressful enough, and I'm still painfully sober."

"I bet the killer left prints on the handle," Eric interjected, his chest puffed proudly as he looked to Rebecca for approval.

"Too bad I didn't pack my fingerprint kit," Maddie said.

"You have a fingerprint kit, cookie?"

"Of course not. I'm a dog walker, not a detective."

"Well I know what someone is getting for Christmas," Dottie said with a little smile.

"Can't wait," she muttered, hoping that she could now return to what she'd been doing.

"What do we do with him?" Eric gestured toward the piano. "It seems wrong to leave him here."

"I doubt he'll steal the silver," Castor drawled.

"Where would we move him to?" Cate asked, ignoring him completely.

"And who's going to move him?" Eric rubbed his lower back, as if to suggest he couldn't possibly help with any physical labor.

"The wine cellar is climate controlled," Carlisle reminded them. "And Helen is already there. It might be the best place to, um, store them."

"I'm not sure that's a good idea. Won't we get in trouble for moving the body?" Florence sounded panicked.

"Not to mention endangering the wine if we lower the temperature." Castor seemed horrified by the concept.

"I think that's the least of our concerns right now. Besides, the local authorities will forgive this one indiscretion, especially when Maddie eliminates the need for a tedious investigation."

"You've got a lot of confidence in a detective who doesn't even have a fingerprint kit," Eric said.

Maddie suppressed an eye roll and turned back to the blood trail, leaving the rest of them to their squabbling. She flipped on the overhead light to combat the gloom from the rapidly darkening sky, and not wanting to miss anything or disturb the evidence, carefully made her way toward the door at the end of the hall. She also noticed paired scuffmarks that occasionally smeared the blood, and about halfway down the hall, there was a small kitchen to the right. "Guess that must be where they make all the tea."

The blood stopped at the door, and Maddie was about to follow it outside when a hand wrapped around her arm. She startled and barely suppressed a scream.

"We need to go back. The storm." Eric gestured at the dark, brooding sky. Menacing clouds scuttled across a field of gray, and the trees bent and swayed in the wind.

"I need to check something first." She tried to open the door, and Eric slammed it shut, just as a thick branch snapped off a nearby striped maple and landed a foot from the door.

"It's not safe. We need to go."

"What about Timothy?"

"Jason has him. Let's go."

Maddie looked from the wildly swaying trees outside to Eric's earnest face. No matter how badly she wanted to follow that trail, hopefully to the spot where Timothy had been murdered, she knew she shouldn't risk her safety—or anyone else's—on the chance that she might find more answers if she went through that back door. Reluctantly, she followed Eric.

"Don't drip blood on my shoes. They've been through enough," Cate whined. Despite the inherent risks to her footwear, she stuck close to Jason, possibly in the hopes that his hulking form would act as a buffer between the weather and her outfit.

Maddie silently thanked the intermittent thunderclaps that interrupted the subsequent harangue on the evils of precipitation. She hung back to avoid the vital shoe talk and was met by Dottie and Carlisle at the door.

"What's your take, hollyhock?"

"Let's see. No one wants me to investigate except for your boyfriend, who is obsessed with studying my nonexistent methodology. I couldn't follow the one legitimate clue I've uncovered thanks to the storm, and there's no reason to believe that whoever played lumberjack with Timothy will hesitate to put an end to my snooping, possibly in some equally violent fashion. My take is that this is hopeless."

Carlisle consulted her watch. "You have just under forty-five hours before the helicopter returns. That should be ample time."

Maddie couldn't even muster a glare.

"Don't be so down on yourself. You're sure to make great progress at tonight's soiree."

"Is this really the best time for a party?"

"The booze, food, and the chef are already on hand. Would you have it all go to waste? Would you prefer we sit around staring at one another, starving, completely sober and waiting for someone else to die?"

"But a party? Two people have died."

"It's not the event I planned for, but I refuse to let the entire weekend go down in flames. There has to be something positive that comes out of it."

"And you think dinner will make up for it?"

"Chef Barbara is a graduate of Le Cordon Bleu," Carlisle explained.

"And what's a pesky double homicide when compared to all that training?" Maddie asked, certain that not even Julia Child could salvage this weekend.

CHAPTER SEVEN

Upon returning to the mansion, Maddie guided Dottie (perhaps more forcefully than necessary) to the third floor. Once they were safely inside her room, she closed the door and fell back against it. Considering how much suspicion surrounded her investigation and the likelihood that it would be clouded by her friendship with Dottie, she hadn't expected it would be so easy for them to secure a private moment. Then again, she also wasn't generally overcome by weather, unlike certain fragile cosmetics divas. Cate seemed to fear precipitation, probably because water had killed her distant relative in the Land of Oz.

Dramatics aside, Cate's shrieking sprint to the mansion had done little more than spur Eric and Castor to similar hydrophobic scampering to safety, leaving the burden of the latest addition to their corpse collection to Jason and Rebecca. Likewise, Florence fled for the security of the mansion, bemoaning her hangover all the while. By the time Maddie and the less delicate faction of the party reached the mansion, the foyer was empty, the others having presumably all headed directly to their rooms in search of dry clothes. Rather than questioning her good fortune, Maddie seized the moment, and grabbing Dottie by the arm, whisked her upstairs.

"Why have you manhandled me into your room, raisin bread?"

"Shh." She pressed her ear against the door, straining to detect signs of activity in the hall.

"And now you're shushing me?"

"Dottie, please. We don't have much time to talk, and we'll have even less if someone finds out that we're having a private conversation."

"Can I at least have a towel? Or must I shiver and drip throughout this clandestine meeting?"

"I don't have a towel."

"Then you should have dragged me to my suite. It has an attached bathroom overflowing with towels."

"Not to mention a party full of people who might come looking for you there. This is safer."

"Paranoia does not become you, poppyseed." She turned in a circle, examining her surroundings with a pout. "How do you not have a towel? Every room was supposed to be fully stocked. I would lodge a complaint with the proprietor, if she hadn't been brutally slain."

"Is this really what you want to focus on right now?"

"It's an injustice. And a rip-off." Dottie stamped her sodden yet elegant foot indignantly just as a sharp, efficient knock signaled the end of their tête-à-tête. Maddie groaned and slumped further.

Dottie nudged her aside and opened the door for a bedraggled yet ever-efficient Carlisle. Despite the rain-spattered glasses that surely obstructed her vision far more than they aided it, she easily maneuvered around her boss and her stupefied friend, her sensible shoes squishing with every step. Carlisle's damp hair hung in limp, soggy, grayish-brown clumps, and water dripped from her chin and clothes. She was the picture of dishevelment, yet she effortlessly tended to Dottie's needs: in one arm, she carried a small stack of fluffy white towels and a silken dressing gown, and with her other hand, she bestowed upon her boss a perfectly garnished martini.

"She's like some kind of robot valet," Maddie muttered into the towel Carlisle offered, reluctantly appreciating her efficiency.

Eschewing whatever modesty she had to begin with, Dottie stripped and delicately patted herself dry before slipping into her robe and wrapping her strawberry-blond locks in another towel. Wondering if this vacation could get any more bizarre, Maddie simply blotted her face, largely to hide from the image of her naked best friend, now emblazoned in her mind.

"What was it you wanted to discuss, mudpuppy?" Dottie asked, her attention already turning to her cocktail.

"Just the double homicide you volunteered me to solve."

"You're not having second thoughts, are you?" She spoke to the mirror as she tackled the rain's damage to her makeup.

Meanwhile, Carlisle retrieved Dottie's discarded clothing from the floor. "I'll do my best to preserve the Dior, Ms. Hunter." She eyed the twill pants critically. "But the damage may be permanent."

"You are a godsend, Carlisle." The woman offered the barest glimpse of a smile through her damp hair veil. "But you're irrigating the hardwood. Have you no other clothes?"

"I came directly from your room." She showed no signs that she regretted her pneumonia-courting shortsightedness. Instead, she stood shivering and dripping on the floor, the added burden of Dottie's rain-soaked attire contributing to the small puddle at her feet.

"Would you like to borrow something?" After the slipper incident the night before, Maddie owed Carlisle.

"Such gallantry, pigeon, but Carlisle would look preposterous in one of your spare ensembles. Besides, how much warmth could your tiny running shorts offer?"

"I was thinking more along the lines of sweatpants and a T-shirt." Dottie shuddered as if she were the one on the verge of hypothermia.

"Thank you." Carlisle accepted the offer and stepped into the closet to disrobe.

"So, what's your take?" Dottie draped herself across Maddie's bed, the burden of the day having taken its toll. "Who's the guilty party?"

"I wish I knew," Maddie sighed, still uncertain she was up to the task. "They all seem to have motive, and since the murders happened overnight, they all had the opportunity."

"*All* of them? Aren't you forgetting that Jason was otherwise occupied last night?"

"Can you be sure he was in the room with you all night? You did sleep, didn't you?"

"Clam sauce, do I look like someone in need of better rest? I never travel without my white noise machine. I slept like the proverbial rock."

"Which means Jason could have slipped out, murdered Helen, killed Timothy, cleaned himself up and been back in bed without disrupting your beauty rest."

"But you're neglecting his stellar character. He's a consummate gentleman, not likely to dispatch a bitter dragon lady, much less the butler."

"I hope you're right."

With obvious reluctance, Carlisle emerged from her modesty corner, looking like the victim of a severe laundry mishap—the sweatpants hit her midcalf, leaving her exceedingly pale calves exposed, and the T-shirt strained across her upper body, like the Hulk midtransformation. She stood awkwardly on the outskirts of the conversation, as if she was lost without the armor of her usual wardrobe.

"Of course I'm right." Dottie pointedly ignored her sturdy assistant's palpable discomfort. "Besides, other than her general unpleasantness, what motive could he possibly have to kill Helen?"

"His movie. She was withholding financing because she didn't want him to have a speaking role."

"That was all a misunderstanding. He assured me he worked out a deal with her."

"For your sake, I hope not. From what he let slip in the guest house, it was something of a casting couch situation."

"Obviously he wasn't going to sleep with her. His tastes are far more refined than Helen."

"I'm sure, but that doesn't help matters much. He still has a strong motive for killing her, even more so if he rejected her advances and saw no way to get his movie made."

"I should take care of these," Carlisle announced as she hoisted the sodden collection of discarded clothes and moved toward the door. "I need to focus my attention on the guests anyway. We don't want them to find the two of you conferring."

"Excellent thinking, Carlisle. Run interference for us. If anyone is looking for me, give us the signal."

"What's the signal?" Maddie asked, wondering if they'd already established some kind of messaging system in case of emergencies. "Is there a secret knock?"

"Yes, Matilda. In the midst of a crisis, Carlisle will take the time to rap the drum solo to 'Wipeout' on the door."

"I see what Cate meant about sarcasm causing wrinkles."

Dottie gasped and rushed to the mirror in a panic.

"If there's any cause for alarm, I'll knock three times, quickly," Carlisle offered.

With that, their eagle-eyed sentinel opened the door a crack, scanned the hallway for any potential witnesses and then slipped from the room.

"I refuse to accept that Jason is a murderer, but I suppose I can see how you might make that mistake. Still, he's far from the only person with a motive to kill Helen."

"Believe me, I know that," Maddie groaned, considering the possible guilty parties yet again.

"Have you considered Florence?" Dottie suggested. "Helen did threaten to fire her."

"True. But do you really think she decided it would be easier to kill her boss than send out a few résumés?"

"Have you never heard of a crime of passion? Her livelihood was in peril, and she'd been embarrassed in front of the entire gathering. An utter humiliation, one that could not be easily dismissed. And knowing Helen, the firing would have come with a healthy dose of denigration. Florence would have been lucky to find a job as a cashier at a drugstore."

"Fine. She has a motive. That still doesn't clear your boyfriend."

"Perhaps not, but you shouldn't be so quick to accuse him when you still have an overflowing pool of suspects. What about Eric? Did you notice how quickly he signed us up to search the stables? Why opt for hay and manure when the perfectly sophisticated teahouse was still on the table, unless he knew there was a body to be found there? He was trying to deflect."

"Or he has an unnatural love of horses."

"A convenient excuse."

"What would his motive be?"

"He and Helen exchanged words last night, moments before your grand entrance. They were headed toward quite the contretemps before Jason intervened."

"What did they argue about?"

"Something to do with horses. I didn't pay attention beyond asking Carlisle and my gallant, and might I add, *innocent* suitor to act as referees."

"Would Carlisle know what the argument was about?"

"Most assuredly. Nothing gets past Carlisle's keen notice."

"Great."

Though it felt a little like she was headed in the wrong direction, Maddie decided to follow up with Carlisle. Given her time constraints, she'd rather be eliminating suspects than bolstering everyone's motives, but she also didn't want to tell Dottie that her future ex-husband was a murderer. "What about Cate? How serious is the potential takeover of her company?"

"Last night was the first I'd heard of it, but it would be catastrophic for Cate."

"How so?"

"She's married to Helen's ex-husband."

"I had surmised as much."

"Well, I'm not one to gossip."

"Of course not."

"But there were rumors of infidelity circulating, and Cate was the featured seductress."

"If that's the case, Helen wouldn't let Cate continue running the company after taking it over. Even if she wasn't responsible for Helen's marriage ending, that's what others believed. Either way, Cate would've been out of a job if Helen had anything to say about it."

"Precisely. And then there's Castor."

"I'll admit he doesn't seem terribly broken up about his twin sister's death, but what reason would he have to murder her?"

"The most powerful motive of all—money. Unlike his sister, Castor couldn't hang onto his fortune if it was superglued to his wallet. The boy has more appreciation for gambling than work. He burned through his trust fund in record time and has been sponging off Helen ever since. Perhaps he grew tired of begging."

"But would he be guaranteed money if she was dead? I wouldn't imagine someone as vindictive and manipulative as Helen would simply hand her fortune over to her brother after her death."

"A valid point but Castor might not have realized that, or he might have hoped the money went back to his parents who adore him." Dottie drained her glass and seemed momentarily surprised when a fresh drink didn't magically appear in her hand. Frowning, she said, "If she wasn't the victim, I would say Helen did it."

"Convenient but not likely."

"What do you think of Rebecca?"

"She doesn't seem to have a motive, but I suppose she could have done it."

"Get your mind out of the murder, butterscotch. I was referring to another role she might play in your life. A weekend romance would do you good."

"In the middle of investigating the killing spree on Murder Island?"

"Does that have to occupy your every thought? Besides, we all know the two of you got sweaty together."

"On a run. There was zero romance involved."

"Why not? She's perfect for you, ocean breeze, and she's clearly interested."

"I doubt that."

"In matters of the heart, I am never wrong, and I can tell she's smitten. Is there any reason you aren't free to pursue other sweaty options with her?"

"Helen and Timothy spring immediately to mind."

"They aren't going to get deader while you have a conversation."

"But someone else might. Who knows how high the body count will climb before this weekend is over?"

Dottie lounged against the headboard and studied Maddie, who desperately fought the urge to squirm under her gaze.

"You aren't still hung up on Dr. Evil, are you?"

Maddie reflected on her most recent romantic disaster. She'd allowed herself to be swept up by intense attraction. That it had been reciprocated had further weakened her judgment, and she'd spent the better part of six months mourning not the loss of the relationship but of her own common sense. And when she wasn't kicking herself for behaving so foolishly, she was accepting that romance, spontaneity, and she didn't mix.

In the future, she would spend more time deciding and much, much less time acting. Not that she was even allowing herself to ponder romantic possibilities, but when they slipped in under the radar, her thoughts were always about a certain kind and charismatic cop who probably didn't remember that Maddie existed. But she wasn't about to admit that to Dottie.

"I promise I'm not thinking about her."

"There's something you aren't telling me. I'll get it out of you, and I'll be sure to remind you of your other, more available options while I get the truth out of you. Meanwhile, what's your plan for ferreting out the murderer?"

"I'm not entirely sure," Maddie sighed, wishing (not for the first time) that she was hunkered down with her dogs instead of enduring the least relaxing weekend getaway in the history of weekend getaways. "For now, it involves getting a closer look at Helen and the wine cellar."

"Biscuit, I must insist that you ready yourself for the evening's festivities."

"That's not on top of my list of priorities right now."

"It should be, honeysuckle. You smell like a gymnasium."

Before Maddie had a chance to respond, three sharp knocks interrupted them.

"We're busted." Dottie sprang from the bed in full secret agent mode. She opened the door the smallest crack possible before peering up and down the hallway. After establishing that the coast was undoubtedly clear, she glanced back at Maddie. "I expect to see you primped, polished and properly dressed for dinner." With that, she slunk into the hallway, leaving Maddie on her own.

Feeling appropriately ridiculous, she followed Dottie's overcautious example, scanning the hallway for activity before slipping out of her room. Thinking it might make for a reasonable cover, she carried her toiletry bag and felt increasingly idiotic as she crept toward the stairs, through the kitchen and into the wine cellar. She encountered no one on her journey, which was both a relief and something of a concern.

At the very least, shouldn't she have passed the maid or the chef? The only path to the wine cellar was through the kitchen, and with Dottie's insistence on a celebratory dinner, that area should have been bustling with gourmet activity. But rather than lingering in the questionable quiet, Maddie offered thanks for whatever small miracle had cleared her path. Not knowing what she expected to find, she descended the stairs.

CHAPTER EIGHT

Once she stood alone in the gloomy wine cellar, Maddie second-guessed her decision to come by herself.

She wasn't afraid, exactly, but she would have been hard-pressed to be less comfortable than she was in this moment. The room seemed much colder and stiller than she remembered. Undoubtedly, the absence of any other living humans added to the chilly atmosphere, and the silence was unsettling. It made sense, of course, but she could honestly say she hoped this would be her last opportunity to spend quality time with a corpse. Thinking it might help to ease herself into the unpalatable undertaking before her, she took a moment to admire the space. Like the rest of the island, it looked like it belonged in an architectural magazine.

Two of the walls were constructed of cobblestone, whether for practical or esthetic reasons Maddie wasn't certain, but the effect was magnificent. The walls exuded an inviting warmth (in direct opposition to the impression created by the corpses currently occupying the space). If not for those unfortunate additions, the walls and floor would easily have complemented the rich woods of the wine racks as well as the table and chairs in the center of the room, which suggested that Helen at least had the capacity (if not the desire) for hospitality.

A Medieval-looking sconce in one of the cobblestone walls cast a dim circle of light that was scarcely enough to see by, and though an overhead light might have been more beneficial for her current purposes, she'd struggled to locate the switch before resorting to the flashlight on her cell phone. Nevertheless, despite its limitations, Maddie appreciated how the soft glow from the sconce added to the cozy setting that Helen had established in her private sanctuary. Maddie imagined the wine cellar must have been a much more inviting space before it became their makeshift morgue.

In a display of decidedly on-the-nose decorating, many of the corners held wine paraphernalia—artificial grapes, wine shadowboxes, wine bottles as candleholders and the like. Several recessed nooks in the adjacent wall were meant to hold individual bottles that were clearly showcase wines, though some of the display nooks sat empty, and Maddie wondered if that was because Helen had yet to fill them…or if there was some other explanation. Had the bottle Helen enjoyed come from one of those spaces or had the killer pilfered a few bottles for him or herself now that Helen could no longer object? Though that seemed a foolish choice—being in possession of part of Helen's wine collection would undoubtedly look suspicious—it wasn't like a murderer could be held up as a model of sound judgment.

Maybe those spaces had never been filled to begin with? It seemed incongruous with Helen's obvious displays of wealth. But perhaps she'd been looking for wildly expensive bottles or some rare vintages to keep there. Maddie was loath to consider just how much money Helen had shelled out simply for the display of luxury beverages. It seemed such a waste.

Shaking her head, she looked to the longest wall, the one opposite the staircase, which was comprised entirely of sturdy wooden wine racks filled almost to capacity with bottles. Maddie imagined the collection amassed there would be, like everything else on the island, ridiculously expensive (and effectively unobtainable for someone in her tax bracket). The final wall was rather unextraordinary aside from featuring yet another portrait of the cellar's owner.

"At least Helen liked Helen," Maddie murmured. "No one else seems to have cared for her."

Suddenly remembering every horror movie she'd ever seen, she wondered again why she'd ever thought this was a good idea. Still, she forced herself to move toward the bodies rather than running back upstairs as her instincts cried out for her to do. She paused at the table where Timothy sat, slumped forward with the ax still in his back, and in spite of his gruesome appearance, she was inordinately pleased to see that Jason hadn't simply dumped him on the floor. His motivation most likely derived from ease and convenience, but she nevertheless appreciated the care evident in his placement. It seemed to her a decision that sprang from compassion, not a trait likely to be found in a murderer on a killing spree. For Dottie's sake, she hoped that was the case. It would certainly make her more agreeable once this weekend was over.

"I'm going to figure out who did this to you," she whispered, determined to make the guilty party pay for this crime.

As motivating as she found his untimely death, she had already learned all she could from his body and now had to focus on the first crime scene of the day. Rushed as she had been upon discovering Helen's body, she had gleaned zero information that would help catch her killer. To be fair, she wasn't even one hundred percent certain that Helen had been murdered, though finding Timothy's body had bolstered her suspicions. She was certainly a prime candidate for murder, and there was no shortage of people on the island who wanted her dead, but beyond that, all Maddie really had was her gut to go on.

Despite the undeniable truth of her current predicament, Maddie couldn't believe that she was standing in probably the most extravagant temporary morgue on the planet, staring at two corpses and preparing to investigate another murder. It was preposterous. She was a dog walker—and a fairly introverted one at that—so how had she ended up in the midst of another murder investigation? Weirder still, why on earth wasn't she wallowing in insecurity?

Not that she was bursting with aplomb—it wasn't like she was any better equipped to catch a killer in this circumstance than when she first stumbled into amateur sleuthing. In fact, considering the ticking clock plus the rising body count, she was due for a good old-fashioned meltdown. Yet she felt oddly calm in the face of overwhelming obstacles. She wouldn't call herself confident. Realistically, her chances of success were so close to nonexistent that they could be called mythical. But (she hesitantly acknowledged) the remote possibility that she might catch the killer *before* her relaxing weekend came to a close had her feeling more enthused than agitated.

"I've definitely been listening to Dottie too much," she muttered before turning her attention to the task at hand.

With the exception of Timothy's presence, the wine cellar seemed very much like it had on her earlier visit to its elusive depths. Having already gotten far too familiar with one corpse that day, she hoped to make quick work of the equally unpleasant task of examining Helen's body for clues, a double perk given the countdown to Dottie's obstinate festivities and her own unkempt state. Though she'd paid more attention to Helen than she preferred upon their initial discovery of her body, she shuddered now at the realization that she would unfortunately have to take an even closer look if she was going to figure out who did this.

"What does it say about me that the only woman I've gotten close to in months is a cadaver?"

Her first glance was at Helen's face, with its open-eyed stare. She noted all the indicators of murder that she'd observed earlier: her eyes were severely bloodshot (had she been alive, she would have made an exemplary "Before" photo in a Visine ad), and her skin was splotchy with what looked like a rash. Maddie didn't know the medical explanation for that, but in conjunction with the bruising and scratches around her neck, it seemed to add up to murder by strangulation. She shivered at the thought of dying in such a horrendous fashion. Just the idea had her clearing her throat and breathing a little deeper.

"If someone was choking me—" She gasped in sudden realization. Helen must have fought back. She was far too domineering to stand idly by as she was attacked.

In an unsettling burst of excitement (followed almost immediately by guilt), Maddie moved to take a closer look at Helen's hands. She didn't hold out hope that, while fighting for her life, Helen had managed to leave some sort of clue that not only would the killer be oblivious to but also that Maddie would then find and understand. Honestly, her chances of finding any clues were minimal at best. And even if she did find something, what was she supposed to do with it? She had neither the skill nor the equipment to analyze her findings. Still, she had to start somewhere.

"I'm so sorry," she whispered to Helen's lifeless form. "I don't like this anymore than you do."

Cringing the entire time, she crouched beside Helen and falteringly turned her cold hand over. There on the floor by her hip was a small red object. "Aha!" Maddie whooped and then caught herself. No matter how thrilling it was to find actual evidence, this was hardly the time or place to celebrate, especially when finding a clue and understanding what it meant were two entirely different beasts.

With tempered excitement, Maddie inspected the object— some kind of pin. She turned it around, trying to make sense of it. Roughly the size of her thumbnail, the pin was one long stick with four smaller twig-like offshoots. From one angle, it looked a bit like a red branch, but viewed from a different angle, it made her think of the windsocks that whipped around trying to attract customers to car washes and dealerships. And while she had no idea why anyone would want that pinned to their clothes, she also didn't find much significance in the world of fashion. Still, it seemed familiar to her, like she'd seen it before but couldn't remember where. The image tugged at her memory, but she couldn't pinpoint its origins. Perhaps Dottie would have a better idea of its significance.

She had to believe that it came from the killer, as it seemed highly unlikely that Helen just happened to collapse onto a random bit of garbage in the middle of the floor in her otherwise immaculate home. There was no dust on the many bottles lining the walls or on the wine racks themselves. The floor was mostly clear of debris—aside from the broken wine glass and an overturned bowl of fake fruit, its artificial produce strewn across the cobblestones. No, the killer had lost this. But what was it? And who did it belong to?

The overhead light snapped on, startling her out of her contemplation and inspiring a flurry of panic. She dropped the pin in her toiletries bag and sprang to her feet. Unless her intruder was Dottie or Carlisle, whoever was bounding down the stairs would be less than happy to find her there.

"Did you get lost on your way to the shower?" Castor's snark did little to hide his shock.

"No, I was just—" She gestured to the wall behind her, having no idea what to say next.

"Lurking in a darkened wine cellar by yourself?"

"I couldn't find the light switch. Though you had no trouble locating it."

"You seem surprised that I'm familiar with my sister's property."

"More that she allowed you in her wine cellar."

"She lacked my expertise. I'm a bit of an oenophile." His smile was closer to a sneer.

"I'm pretty sure she didn't call you down here now."

"No. That was my hankering for a superb bottle." He plucked a bottle from a nearby rack. "A complex and full-bodied cabernet franc. I'm in."

"Doesn't it bother you at all that your sister is dead?"

"What can I say? We weren't close." He glanced up from the bottle he ogled. "You still haven't explained what you're doing here. This *is* a crime scene."

"For a murder that I've been asked to investigate."

"Against almost everyone's wishes," he reminded her.

"I was just leaving." She headed toward the stairs but paused at the bottom. "Coming?" she asked Castor. "As you said, it's a crime scene."

"Right you are." He grabbed a second bottle and followed her up the stairs where Dottie was waiting for her.

Dottie stepped close to Castor, an invasion of his personal space that didn't seem to bother him in the least. She touched his shoulder before letting her hand wander down his chest, and with her voice dropped to a husky near-whisper, she asked, "Castor, love, could you give me a moment alone with my dear friend?"

Appropriately spun, Castor laughed nervously before kissing Dottie's hand and departing. Before Maddie could speak, Dottie dragged her farther into the kitchen.

"We have another problem. The chef is dead."

"Murdered?"

"See for yourself."

Carlisle, who had been standing guard at the pantry door, stepped aside to reveal Chef Barbara sprawled across a giant sack of flour. A bloody marble rolling pin lay on the floor beside her head, which was the obvious source of the blood.

"So, I'm going to need you to prepare dinner."

"*That's* your priority?"

"Need I remind you of my already disgruntled guests? I can't let them go hungry on top of exposing them to a killer."

"Because that's the worst thing that could happen this weekend."

"Pardon me for thinking of my guests' needs."

"Okay, but I'm a little busy solving a murder. Or three. Why doesn't Carlisle cook while I try to find a killer before anyone else dies?"

"Are you suggesting that I'm not busy?" Carlisle asked peevishly.

"Or maybe we could just eat sandwiches?" Maddie suggested, hoping to avoid a sharp blow to the head from Carlisle's clipboard.

"This will not be remembered as the event where Gwendolyn Hunter lost her senses and served sandwiches." The word sounded foul on Dottie's tongue.

"I'm sure it won't be," Maddie muttered.

"What's the problem, crostata? I've dined at your home more than once, so I know you can find your way around a kitchen. And your grandmother is a first-rate chef. Surely the apple galette didn't fall far from the tree."

"But I've never cooked a gourmet meal, certainly not for a crowd this size."

"You can have Carlisle for a sous chef." At that pronouncement, Carlisle's eyes grew wide, and she seemed on the verge of insubordination.

"But how does this help me solve these murders?"

"The element of surprise," Dottie proclaimed, as if she had a valid and irrefutable point. "Whoever dispatched the chef won't be expecting a five-course meal."

"Five courses?" Maddie shrieked.

"Soup, salad, palate cleanser, entrée and dessert. Whoever reacts with shock is our assassin."

"Unless they know how determined you are."

"In that case, at least you'll have had a chance to discuss the case with Carlisle during your arduous meal prep. She's an excellent sounding board." Dottie stepped back and frowned, giving Maddie false hope that she might reconsider this plan. "The only drawback is that you can't wear the designer frock I set out for you. We can't have you slaving away in couture."

"At last, a bright side," she muttered as her friend ushered her toward the stairs.

"Carlisle will get started in here while you get cleaned up. By the time you're presentable, I'll have found the perfect ensemble."

"Terrific."

CHAPTER NINE

"I swear I was only gone twenty minutes," Maddie said as she surveyed the results of her reluctant sous chef's confusing approach to meal prep.

Left to her own devices, Carlisle had divested the refrigerator and freezer of their contents, overloading the counters, island and table with every conceivable cold ingredient, condiments included. She stood frowning at the array of foodstuffs she'd amassed, as if she expected them to whip themselves into a delectable feast at her will. If not for the mess they'd have to wade through just to get started on the failure that was destined to be their culinary collaboration, Maddie would have been tickled at discovering an area in which Carlisle, apparently, did not excel.

If not for her losing battle with Dottie about the wisdom of cooking in a sequined ballgown (the plunging neckline of which elevated her discomfort to staggering heights), Maddie might have returned in time to stop this. Instead, she now stood in the middle of a kitchen that had been turned inside out, sequins shimmering as she spun around scanning the room for an apron or a way out of this mess.

"I've conducted a thorough inventory of the refrigerator." Carlisle spoke to her notes rather than Maddie.

She was astounded at the order Carlisle had once again imposed on a chaotic situation—more evidence for her robot theory. However, the fact that her efficiency had also created an enormous, perishable roadblock was something of a drawback. They'd effectively have to clean the kitchen in order to get started on cooking dinner, and based on Dottie's grandiose plan (married to the condensed timeline for accomplishing the task), they did not have time. She felt like a contestant on some cooking show, but without the celebrity judge or potential for a prize. Here, her only reward would be a mollified Dottie, which, to be fair, could be worth gold.

"I can see how you would have to empty the refrigerator to do that."

Carlisle glared at her but opted not to explain her thought process further.

"It's an interesting approach, but speaking for myself, I find it easier to prepare a meal if I get out only what I need, which incidentally, might include a few items from the pantry. Really, canned goods aren't just for the poor and despondent anymore."

"We might access those rebranded canned goods if not for the dead chef currently blocking them." She pointed to the latest in their ever-growing collection of bodies. "Unless you wanted to crawl over Chef Barbara like she's human monkey bars, but you might want to save the acrobatics, given your outfit and your track record with coordination this weekend."

Maddie again lamented the limitations of her Dottie-approved fashion. Though she didn't look forward to the experience at all, she imagined that her sequined torture would add an extra challenge to relocating the chef's body.

"I don't suppose we could ask Jason to help us move her?"

"Not without losing the element of surprise."

"Because common sense and logic won't take care of that on their own." Resigned to the task at hand, she bent to grab Chef

Barbara under the arms, cringing at the sight of the congealing blood. "But if he is the guilty party, he really should have to help."

With Carlisle at the feet, they hoisted Barbara from her floury resting place, and groaning under the weight of their shared burden, they tried to move through the doorway simultaneously, an action that sent Maddie and Chef Barbara's upper body ricocheting off the doorjamb and into a shelf of legumes.

"Do you think he could have done it?" Maddie asked after righting herself and allowing Carlisle to exit first. They lumbered toward the stairs to the wine cellar at a pace that wouldn't guarantee they'd reach their destination before Arbor Day.

Carlisle grumbled as they inched along, her breathing labored, and she occasionally glanced over her shoulder toward their destination (which seemed to be as far from them as when they began their torturously slow journey a year earlier).

"I think it's certainly possible," she huffed, pausing their painful progress to catch her breath. "But it would be better for everyone involved if he's innocent."

"Because Dottie will take it badly?" Maddie wondered how disrespectful it would be to drag the chef the rest of the way to the stairs.

"I was thinking more that the rest of us have almost no chance of defending ourselves against him in a fight, and if memory serves, your investigations are seldom peaceful affairs."

Maddie stumbled and almost lost her grip but managed to avoid dropping the chef and sending her shooting across the freshly waxed floor and down the stairs like a human toboggan. Much as she hated to admit it, Carlisle had a point. In one hundred percent of her murder investigations, she'd had violent confrontations with killers. That, in itself, was a damning predicament, but in this instance, Jason (if he was the killer) not only was well-muscled and a fighter by trade (even if it was pretend fighting), but also had backup in the form of his physically fit and loyal sister.

"But if he's not the killer, he'll make one hell of an ally."

By the time they began their descent to the wine cellar, Maddie's muscles were crying out in pain. She wasn't sure how much longer she could hang on to their load. Carlisle, leading the charge, looked equally fatigued but determined to tough it out, gravity be damned.

"Have you ever considered avoiding violence altogether?"

"It's not like I go looking for physical altercations."

"Yet they find you."

Maddie groaned as they reached the blessed end of the staircase and deposited Chef Barbara in the East Coast's most well-appointed provisional catacomb. She briefly considered placing her at the table with Timothy, but at the rate the killer was going, they would run out of seats before they ran out of corpses. Better to leave her on the floor and try to prevent adding any more occupants.

Back in the kitchen, Carlisle reverted to methodical robot form. "As I was saying before that disagreeable diversion, I have good news. Thanks to Chef Barbara's obvious appreciation for efficiency, she completed much of the prep work for tonight's meal before…" She nodded toward the pantry, apparently unable to verbalize their latest loss. "So that will save us some time, and at least a portion of the meal will live up to our guests' expectations."

Maddie ignored the subtle dig at her cooking skills, focusing instead on her near-euphoric relief at the news that she wouldn't have to create an elaborate five-course meal from scratch. Upon her designation as the replacement chef, a knot of tension had settled between her shoulder blades and had been growing in strength ever since. But now it loosened. She still had no faith that she could pull off a sophisticated meal for a dinner party of elites who probably dined at Michelin-starred restaurants as often as she ate leftovers, but at least now she held out hope that her attempt wouldn't be an utter fiasco—until she considered Carlisle's statement more fully.

"I don't suppose this is one of those times when good news doesn't go hand in hand with bad news."

"Alas, no. The bad news is that I don't know what most of this is supposed to be."

"But that's like having no good news." Maddie felt like crying. "Unidentifiable prep work is a tease. It's worse than no prep work at all."

"Not *all* of it is unidentifiable," Carlisle huffed in defense of her essentially useless efforts thus far.

"So tell me what's identifiable." She resisted the urge to sink to the floor in despair.

Carlisle grabbed a large stainless-steel bowl and held it aloft like a prize. "I believe this is a salad."

"A salad?" Maddie glanced into the bowl. It contained spring greens and little else. "Thank god we won't have to wash or tear lettuce. That's a real time saver." Carlisle glared at her, clearly irritated. "You don't cook much, do you?"

"It's not one of my strengths." She pursed her lips in disapproval.

"Is there anything else that you recognize?"

"I think I found dessert, or at least part of it." She proudly displayed a mixing bowl containing a frothy egg white mixture, its stiff peaks glossy under the harsh kitchen lights. But meringue by itself wasn't much of a discovery, if that's what this even was.

Maddie wished, not for the first time, that she could call her grandmother. If anyone could talk her through this fiasco of an evening, it was Granny Doyle. If only she had a portion of Granny's aplomb, then the simple act of preparing dinner wouldn't seem so daunting. Assuming they survived this weekend, Maddie was determined to spend more time with her grandmother—maybe some of her self-assurance would rub off. But first, she had to get through Dottie's holiday on Assassination Isle.

Hopeful for some legitimate good news, she pointed to a container near the edge of the island. "What's this?"

"Possibly a sauce?" Carlisle grimaced at the contents of the bowl. "It's green."

Maddie, deciding that she'd need more certainty than Chef Carlisle's best guess, sniffed at the bowl and frowned. "It even smells green."

Carlisle hesitated before inhaling delicately at the lip of the dish. "Perhaps we'll just set this aside for now."

"Good plan. Is there anything that could be considered an entrée?"

"Nothing you'll like." She pointed to a plate of fileted halibut. "I know you have reservations about seafood."

"Only because it keeps trying to kill me."

"Not all seafood is crustaceans."

"That's not as comforting as you might think. Did Chef Barbara leave us anything else?"

"A second dessert." She opened the freezer to reveal the entirety of its holdings: a tub of sorbet, alarmingly orange in color. Dismayed by its startling hue, Maddie again sniffed and, feeling reasonably confident there would be no hidden shellfish in sorbet, risked sampling the dish in question, pleased to discover its light mango flavor.

"Aside from that, we seem to be on our own."

"Not to belittle your super thorough and not at all pointless inventory, but what are we supposed to do with two desserts, an incomplete salad and an entrée that you don't know how to prepare and I'm afraid to touch?"

"*Pointless* inventory?"

"You're right. It's terrific to know just how completely screwed we are. I'm so glad you spent time making notes on your stupid clipboard instead of trying to find a recipe of some kind. You do know what a recipe is, don't you?"

Carlisle's mouth fell open, and Maddie worried for a moment that in lieu of a lambasting, the assistant might simply resort to violence. In a huff, she picked up the salad and spun toward the refrigerator just as Maddie grabbed the mystery sauce. Their arms collided, and time slowed as the bowl slipped from Maddie's hands, flipped in the air and sent a pale green liquid cascading through the air. Miraculously, neither of them was hit by the explosive fountain of sauce, but whatever it had been was no longer part of the menu. Worse, in her haste not to be doused with liquid of an undetermined nature, Maddie leapt away from the arc, knocking the bowl of meringue with her elbow and sending it crashing to the floor.

As the metallic clang of the bowls clattering against the marble floor knelled their defeat, Maddie looked up to see Carlisle's appalled expression just as the platter of fish on the edge of the island wavered precariously for a moment before losing the battle with gravity.

For one eternal moment as the clamor died down, they stared at one another in horrified disbelief.

"Any chance Dottie will be satisfied with a four-course dinner? Maybe we can substitute cocktails for the entrée. She'll love it."

"What did you do?" Carlisle whispered.

"Avoided a nightmarish dry-cleaning bill?"

"I can't believe you just did that." She simply stared at the unsalvageable meal at their feet. She either hadn't noticed or didn't care about the glob of meringue on the toe of her left shoe.

"Well, I was hoping to waste even more time in the kitchen when I should be trying to catch a murderer."

"Perhaps if you were more efficient, you'd have a better idea of who did it. It's not like you have an endless pool of suspects. There are literally thirteen people on this island, three of whom are dead. How hard could it be?"

"Fine. I've figured it out. You're the murderer." She heard her voice rising in anger. "Let me just lock you in the wine cellar with your kills until the police can get here, and then I can focus on this ridiculous dinner."

"If I had murdered anyone, I would have started with you." Carlisle's volume rose to match Maddie's. "And this *ridiculous dinner* is an elegant affair, or it would be if an uncouth barbarian wasn't in charge of it."

"What is going on in here?" Dottie glowered at them from the doorway. "I wanted a simple, five-course dinner, not WrestleMania."

"You should probably check with Jason before you rule it out."

Dottie merely glared at her best friend before her eyes zeroed in on the green puddle at Carlisle's feet. "Is that Chef Barbara's world-famous chilled spring English pea soup?"

"Or possibly a sauce."

"I expect this level of destruction from Matilda, but Carlisle, you were supposed to be a good influence. I had hoped you were above such misconduct."

"It's not Carlisle's fault. Not entirely. We have completely incompatible work styles."

"I suggest you rise above them long enough to prepare a meal. Assuming any provisions survived your brief tenure in the kitchen."

"We have salad." Carlisle still cradled the bowl of greens like an infant. Her voice sounded small and timid, and she seemed to have shrunk about half a foot.

"Just a thought, I've read that Europeans are moving toward the one-course meal. It's all the rage in Paris."

"Thanks for the advice, sweetbreads, but this weekend has already seen enough disasters. I don't need to voluntarily sabotage it and my reputation by consulting you on trends."

"But with the time constraints and this mess to clean up, I'm just not sure—"

"My guests are already aggrieved. They were promised elegance and relaxation, a delightful repose from the day-to-day pressures of life."

"I guess I severely underestimated the burden of wealthy entitlement."

"Just because you've made yourself the poster girl of the working class, Matilda, don't think that erases your own entitled youth. You didn't grow up eating government cheese and mastering the art of thrift store fashion or navigating food pantries. I wouldn't dare suggest that you shouldn't be proud of your accomplishments, but in addition to having rich parents who can rescue you if your luxury business fails, you've also readily accepted my help in cultivating your clientele. So kindly stop acting superior to those who aren't ashamed of the wealth they take full advantage of."

Though there was a stratosphere of difference between Maddie's comfortably upper-class upbringing and the one percent club Dottie surrounded herself with, she knew her friend had a point. And even if she didn't, complaining about spoiled entitlement as she stood in the state-of-the-art kitchen of a sprawling mansion on a private island, wearing designer clothes she hadn't paid for on a vacation that had cost her nothing was the pinnacle of hypocrisy.

"You're right. I'm sorry."

"Try to remember that more often, pumpkin." She ran a hand over her elegant-as-usual dress, almost as if she could wipe away the distress of her current situation as easily as ridding herself of wrinkles. "This meal is going to be the saving grace of this entire excursion. My guests are all on edge right now, a condition not helped by their extreme hunger."

"Cocktail hour with a killer probably isn't helping either," Maddie grumbled.

"I need less fighting and more cooking. Perhaps you could try communicating, both about the menu and the case, and to be clear, you need to make it elegant, and you need to hurry. Eric was on the hunt for board games when your cacophony demanded my attention."

"Well, there's nothing like Parcheesi to take your mind off a serial murderer." Maddie shifted to obscure the messy truth about the saving grace of Dottie's weekend. The less she knew about the dire state of her elegant meal, the better.

"Good news!" Eric's enthusiastic voice carried from the other side of the door. "I found Clue in one of the closets. Hurry back so we can get started."

"This weekend is in rapid decline." Dottie sighed heartily but seemed to accept her mundane fate. "I'm Miss Scarlet," she declared as she exited the kitchen.

"This is not the worst thing that could happen," Maddie said once the door closed behind their demanding sponsor.

"Really? It looks pretty bad from where I'm standing," Carlisle said. "We have a dead chef, an unsalvageable meal to clean up, a hungry crowd, a murderer on the loose and an irate boss. How is this situation salvageable?"

"Well, she's not my boss, so that's something."

Carlisle looked close to tears, a development almost as unsettling as the thought of spending the night with a killer among them.

"We can fix this," Maddie assured her co-chef and darted to the pantry, careful to avoid the blood-stained patch of floor.

With half her mind on dinner and the other on the enterprising murderer among them, she scanned the shelves without any real hope that she would find a miracle in the form of a fast, easy back-up meal that required neither the knowledge nor the skillset of a professional chef. Even if they hadn't undone Chef Barbara's hard work, she doubted she could have produced a five-course meal that lived up to Dottie's standards. Now that she had to start from scratch? She would need the ghost of Julia Child to guide her through this endeavor.

The top shelf held a wealth of spices—quite possibly every seasoning imaginable. If only humans could survive on Turkish bay leaves and tarragon alone, they'd be set. Below the well-accoutred spice shelf, she found innumerable nonperishables—enough organic packaged goods to start a high-end grocery store—but without a recipe or her grandmother to guide her, they and the spices above them were essentially useless. In most areas of her life, Maddie was not a "wing it" kind of girl, a designation that absolutely extended to cooking, especially when her only help came in the form of a clipboard-wielding kitchen neophyte.

"I wish I could call Granny," she groaned to a shelf overflowing with canned vegetables. "She'd know what to do."

As she stood with her hand resting on a can of refried beans, contemplating the likely repercussions of serving taco dip as an entrée, she spotted a familiar package tucked behind a box of organic ziti. She felt a disproportionate degree of bliss at the sight of the spoon-holding, four-fingered Hamburger Helper mascot smiling and waving to her from the shelf like a beacon of hope.

"Perfect," she said, already dreading the reaction to what she was about to do. "We're in luck. There's Hamburger Helper," she proclaimed as she emerged victorious from the pantry.

"And you're happy about this? We need an epicurean feast, not boxed despair," Carlisle gasped.

"It's not dinner at Alinea, but it will take care of our hungry guest problem."

"You can't. Ms. Hunter would never serve that."

"She will if she wants us to serve more than salad and dessert. We got lucky with the Hamburger Helper."

"Interesting interpretation of luck."

"I'm going to see what other treasures I can find in the pantry. Maybe there's some Spam lurking behind the quinoa."

"Ms. Hunter won't like it," Carlisle sniffed. "She doesn't eat the food of the downtrodden."

"She'll never know." Carlisle looked doubtful. "Because your job is to come up with gourmet-sounding names for what I serve and to keep Dottie's glass full."

Carlisle frowned for a moment, obviously debating what to do. Then she nodded once and began tidying up the remnants of Chef Barbara's work. "We'll call the main course *boeuf le roturier*," she said as she dabbed at the rapidly spreading green goo with a plenitude of paper towels.

"Of course, you speak French."

Their plan in place, Maddie dashed back into the pantry. Though she had no time to conduct a thorough search of the crime scene, it seemed a wasted opportunity not to at least perform a cursory examination. Since most of the guests were engrossed in a classic (if all-too fitting) board game, it might be her only chance to inspect the scene without the input of the sleuth committee. Maybe she'd get lucky and find a signed confession or the killer's name written in Chef Barbara's blood.

But as soon as she passed the threshold, her foot bumped something, sending it skittering across the floor. She looked down in time to see the bloody murder weapon roll to a stop against the opposite wall.

"That probably wasn't helpful," she muttered, debating the wisdom of moving the rolling pin somewhere safer (and where she wouldn't have to see it). Considering how often she and her wildly unqualified sous chef would be in and out of the crime scene, no evidence would be safe there. But what if relocating it damaged it?

Though it was a bit late to worry about that now, she supposed. How much more damage could she do by stashing it in a Ziplock than she already had by kicking it across the pantry? And assuming they didn't all succumb to the killer before the weekend was over, she would be better off preserving what little evidence they had. The weapon and the murder had been one of opportunity, meaning there was a chance that the killer had left fingerprints. On the off chance that she hadn't already rendered them unusable, she carefully secured the rolling pin in a freezer bag, but then she was left wondering where exactly one stored a used murder weapon. Somehow, she doubted that a thirteen-bedroom mansion with a wine cellar, stables, a guesthouse and a teahouse also included an evidence locker. Maybe Carlisle had some insights on the matter—her skillset was diverse and surprising.

"What do you know about storing evidence?"

"More than I know about cooking." She blinked several times at the bag Maddie held.

"Where do you think we should put this?"

"Did you photograph it before moving it?"

"For what? The world's grisliest scrapbook?"

"Or the police, who might need to establish a chain of evidence."

"Oh." Maddie bit her lip, wishing she'd consulted Carlisle two minutes earlier. "I didn't think of that. Not that I had time to snap a pic before I kicked it on my way into the pantry."

"Did you at least avoid putting your fingerprints all over it?"

"Yes, mother, I managed not to incriminate myself. Now, what do we do with it?"

"How are you the detective?" Impatiently, she grabbed the bag and stowed it in the freezer, just above the sorbet that Maddie now had no intention of eating.

"It wasn't my idea to have me investigate. Believe me, I'd much rather be home with my dogs and a good book, but since we're here, we might as well do our best to survive and then discourage Dottie from planning any more vacations."

"She means well, you know."

"Of course I do," Maddie snapped.

She'd known Dottie for years and understood exactly how her best friend's mind functioned. Even before she had money, Dottie always had refined tastes. Just because she hadn't been able to afford the finer things then, didn't mean she settled for inferior experiences. And now that she had the means for the elegance she'd always appreciated? She was aggressively cosmopolitan. But maybe that wasn't what Carlisle meant.

"What, specifically, is she so well-meaning about now?"

Carlisle was on the verge of a smile, an unsettling but not altogether terrible turn of events. Maddie supposed it wouldn't be the worst thing in the world to get along with Dottie's lackey, which probably meant she should no longer refer to her as such.

"She worries about you being alone and that you'll never meet anyone special if you spend all of your time with dogs."

"So she traps me on an island with a murderer?"

"No. She trapped you on an island with a suitable mate, an expensive wardrobe and the hope that circumstance and fate would take care of the rest. And if that didn't work, the bar is fully stocked."

Maddie played over what Carlisle just said as she pushed the ground beef around the skillet. Dottie had always taken too much interest in Maddie's love life (or lack thereof), so it wasn't unusual for her to give Cupid a push every now and then.

"Did she plan this weekend for me?"

"Not exactly." She seemed to be weighing her answer carefully. "Ms. Hunter's motivations were multifaceted, but your situation was an influencing factor. Once she learned that Jason's sister was also a lesbian, she encouraged him to bring her along." Maddie rolled her eyes at her friend's well-intentioned machinations. "She thought it would be good for you to meet someone."

"I'm not interested in meeting anyone."

"She had noticed that. Hence the weekend getaway."

"I have more important things to worry about than finding a girlfriend, like catching a murderer."

"And what about the remaining ninety-five percent of your life, when you haven't stumbled into a murder investigation?"

If she hadn't been willing to discuss her lackluster love life with Dottie, there was no way she was going to open up to Carlisle. Out of necessity, they'd established something of a truce, but that didn't entitle Carlisle to know all of her secrets. Instead of answering she deflected, as usual.

"Dottie said you overheard the argument that Helen had with Eric last night."

"Everyone did. But when I first heard them, they were discussing Pharoah."

"Am I supposed to know who that is?"

"That is a horse in the rescue that Mr. Dillingham funds. I believe he was trying to convince Ms. Andreas to adopt Pharoah."

"I thought he loved horses. Why would he willingly subject one to Helen?"

"She takes excellent care of her property. Perhaps he thought the animal would fall under that heading, and by extension, be well cared for by her staff."

"I guess that explains Eric's thinking, but what was in it for Helen?"

"It seems she was looking to expand her holdings into the equine arena. I surmise the move was motivated more by status than any genuine appreciation for the animals or their care. My understanding is that she often prioritized status over other considerations. Perhaps that's why she was so infuriated with Eric for trying to, and I quote, 'pawn off one of his broken beasts,' end quote. Apparently, Helen had been working with a dealer of less than reputable ethics when Eric brought Pharoah to her attention. Why he thought a questionable home for a horse in need would be a wise choice is a question I can't answer."

"But he's a horse lover worth millions—"

"He's worth billions, with a b."

"Of course he is. But that's even more reason to expect that he could have given Pharaoh a home rather than subjecting him to life with Helen. He should have been relieved that Helen backed out, not angry. It doesn't seem like a very strong motive for murder."

"In typical Helen fashion, or so I gather, she threatened to sue him and his rescue. The publicity, even from a baseless lawsuit could have destroyed the organization."

"Jeopardizing all of those horses. That would be more than enough reason for Eric to want her gone."

Maddie rolled over this new information as she stirred the sauce mix and pasta with the ground beef. She could certainly understand Eric's desire to do the right thing, though she still couldn't comprehend how putting any living creature in Helen's care could be construed as "the right thing." And she was all too familiar with his commitment to animals—she hadn't built a minor pet care empire out of extreme disinterest in animals and their well-being. She herself had intervened more than once on an animal's behalf, and despite some scary encounters as a result, she doubted she would stop advocating for animals anytime soon. But would she murder someone for endangering an animal? She didn't think so. But of all the motives she'd heard for wanting Helen dead, Eric's was the only one she could come close to sympathizing with.

Still, no matter how much Helen may have had it coming, Timothy and Chef Barbara did not, and whoever was responsible was going to pay.

CHAPTER TEN

The mood in the dining room was surprisingly upbeat when they sat down to eat. Whether that was thanks to Dottie's liberal approach to bartending or the ameliorating effects of board games, Maddie didn't know. Whatever the cause, she was relieved when no one immediately rebuked her mealtime collaboration with Carlisle. It was a rare positive experience in an overall abominable weekend.

It started well, with all of the guests responding favorably to Carlisle's cherished salad. In a somewhat uninspired display of culinary resourcefulness, Maddie had complemented the mixed greens with some tomatoes, croutons and a balsamic vinaigrette that Chef Barbara may or may not have intended for that purpose. Though praise for the slapdash menu was hardly warranted, Jason complimented every forkful he shoveled into his mouth. Maddie doubted that dressed up roughage could so thoroughly satisfy a man whose caloric consumption per meal equaled her daily allowance, but she supposed that as long as Jason was happy, Dottie would be happy, a theory that was tested by her unpleasantly surprised reaction to the appetizer Maddie had concocted from Spam, cheddar cheese and biscuit mix.

The other guests, however, lacked Jason's enthusiasm for the meal and turned to other, less friendly topics.

"Should we assume that you've been too busy cooking to frame one of us for murder?" Cate's unwavering eye contact as she stabbed a Spam puff with her fork was unsettling at best.

"Why would you think I was cooking? That's what Chef Barbara was hired for."

"For starters, you weren't in the lounge with the rest of us, and so far this meal has been a little more Olive Garden than Ina Garten. Also, you're wearing an apron. Unless you're trying to spark a new fashion trend—which I wouldn't encourage— you're probably the one responsible for this curious mélange of flavors."

"Just wait for the entrée," she muttered, not at all surprised that Dottie's ruse fooled no one.

"Well, I appreciate a good cook." Rebecca licked her lips appreciatively, and Maddie felt an unsettling warmth radiating from her chest.

"I'm an excellent chef." Eric grinned from across the table.

"What's your signature dish? Oats and hay?" Rebecca asked.

"Why didn't Chef Barbara make dinner?" Castor interrupted the uncomfortably one-sided flirting.

"She's indisposed at the moment." Dottie drained her martini with an air of finality, and Carlisle, who had only recently returned to her seat after serving the second course, rose to address the deficiency.

"What do you mean 'indisposed'?" Florence, looking marginally better than she had that morning, asked. "Is that code for dead?" Everyone turned to stare at her. "As if you weren't all wondering the same thing. Someone seems to die every twelve hours on this wretched island. It's not an illogical assumption."

"But if she died, shouldn't we have been informed?" Cate said, her voice shriller than usual.

"You had plans to mourn the chef?" Castor spoke into his wineglass.

"I just find it highly suspicious that we were kept in the dark about a murder. It's bad enough to be trapped with a killer. We should at least be informed."

"Really, Gwendolyn, we should have been told." Eric puffed out his chest as if he were David to Dottie's Goliath.

"And what would you have done had you known?" Dottie threw her arms out in her frustration, allowing Carlisle to slip a fresh cocktail into her hand.

"I might have suggested we play Monopoly instead."

"You're a true gentleman. What about the rest of you? Would any of you have done anything differently had you known about the chef's murder?"

"Yes," Cate screeched. "I would have hidden in my room. I told you all that we should take cover until this weekend is over, but no one wanted to listen. Our lives are at risk, and I have no interest in this island being my final resting place."

"I'm sure someone would ship you back home for burial," Castor said.

"How reassuring."

"Personally, I would have liked to watch the detective at work." Jason chomped down on his fourth Spam puff, grinning appreciatively, and Maddie pondered whether the satisfaction of telling Dottie about her conquest's unrefined tastes was worth the certain backlash of exposing her guests to the horrors of canned meats.

"You know, the beefcake is right. I would have liked that too." Castor turned his attention on Maddie. "Tell us, Shar-Pei Sherlock, what have you discovered today?"

"Nothing definitive." She shrugged. Even if she had a better idea of who the guilty party was, she saw no benefit to revealing her progress to the very people she was investigating.

"You've been investigating all day and don't have a single clue to show for it?" Florence's skepticism was nearly palpable.

"Not all day." Rebecca roared to her defense. "She did make dinner, which is delicious by the way."

"Can we at least know how she died?" Cate spared Maddie from the reciprocal flirting expected of her (if not by Rebecca then most assuredly by the sponsor of this lamentable holiday).

"What difference does it make? Do you have a murder bingo card or something?" Rebecca asked.

"I just like to be informed."

"How do we know you aren't already informed?" Florence asked. "Maybe you know exactly what happened to the chef because you're the one who did it?"

"When would I have had the chance? I was with you all from dawn to dusk."

"Except after we got back from the teahouse," Eric pointed out. "We all went to our rooms to change. You might have snuck out and killed the chef while we were all otherwise occupied."

"And still achieved this look?" She gestured to her flawless hair, makeup, and dress. "It's much more likely that you squeezed in a murder between the monsoon and board games in the lounge. It's not as if you spent any time grooming."

"It's time for the next course," Carlisle announced. She stood to Dottie's left, prepared to foist un-haute cuisine on the party whether they were ready for it or not.

"Why is Carlisle serving dinner?" Cate asked.

"Because the butler was murdered and I reject family-style dining," Dottie replied.

"What about the maid?" Florence asked. "Wouldn't she be the next logical choice?"

"Unless she was murdered too," Castor said.

"My god, he's right," Florence squawked. "The maid is dead, isn't she?"

"Of course not." Carlisle's customary confidence was noticeably absent.

"That sounded convincing," Rebecca said.

"Are you thinking what I'm thinking?" Castor asked.

"That I shouldn't have wasted all that time cooking?" Maddie grumbled.

"Or that he should have placed bets on who would survive the weekend," Cate deadpanned.

"Good idea. I'll keep it in mind for our next gathering."

"We need to make sure the maid hasn't been killed," Jason said, the sobriety of his statement amplified by the fact that he put down his fork.

"There's no cause for alarm." Carlisle clutched the handle of the serving cart tightly. "Leslie has simply locked herself in her room."

"I'll go knock on her door to make sure she's all right," Jason offered.

"Hold on there, big fella." Castor rose to stop him. "You aren't going alone."

"Heroism from Castor? I'm shocked," Cate sneered.

"How much courage does it take to knock on a door?"

"More like common sense, Catie." Castor, like everyone else, ignored Eric's remark. "What if he's the killer? The last thing we should do is send him to pay a visit to his next victim alone."

"Unless he already killed her." Eric earned a scowl from Rebecca.

"Why would I kill the maid?"

"Unfluffed pillows? Subpar hospital corners? Maybe she gave you skim milk for your bowl of Wheaties. I wouldn't really know what would inspire a deranged killer," Castor said.

"I'm not a deranged killer."

"What kind of killer are you?" Florence asked.

"I'm not any kind of killer," Jason protested.

"Perhaps we should all check on the maid." Dottie sighed. "I'm sure we'll be more inclined to enjoy this…feast once we ascertain an accurate body count."

The commotion of their collective departure roused the trio of dogs who (in spite of the aneurism such unrefined behavior was sure to cause Dottie) had been slumbering at Maddie's feet beneath the dining room table. One by one, they shook the sleep from their furry frames and barreled out the door, ready for whatever adventure was about to take place. Ares, dwarfed by his massive companions, compensated for his small stature by spinning and barking in the direction of the pack of torturously slow humans. His shrill yaps pierced the air, adding to the general tumult.

"Are we really doing this again?" Cate asked as they raced toward the grand staircase.

"What? Showing compassion for someone below your tax bracket?" Rebecca asked.

"Oh, because I'm wealthy I'm some kind of unfeeling monster?"

"*I'm* not the one who said it."

"Maybe we could focus on this after we find Leslie," Maddie said, nudging Cate and Rebecca back to the matter at hand.

"Why wait? I can multitask. It's probably what led to my successful career as a callous rich person."

"Let it go, Cate, lest we start to think Rebecca is right about you. And don't you dare mention how diplomacy leads to wrinkles."

Their collective ascent to the third floor was hindered by two hundred and ten pounds of enthused dogs underfoot as well as the impracticality of designer garments for vigorous movement. It also didn't help that certain members of their party had roughly the same interest in checking on the maid as they did in double coupon day.

"Why are we running?" Florence panted as she brought up the rear.

"It's an emergency," Jason barked and continued taking the stairs two at a time. He and the dogs had already reached the second landing.

"How so? Either the maid is already dead and there's nothing we can do, or the killer is part of this group, so she's safe."

"The lady has a point." Castor slowed his gait considerably, a measure soon copied by Eric.

"But if we let the dog-walking detective beat us to the scene, she could paint it to make any of us look guilty." Cate, who seemed to be in possession of an endless supply of footwear not intended for actual movement, paused on the landing to the second floor to adjust her shoes.

"You're irritatingly paranoid, Cate."

"But not necessarily wrong," Eric pointed out.

"I hate you all," Florence grumbled as they resumed their collective beeline to the maid's locked door.

One by one, as the guests reached the top of the stairs, they were met by three panting pooches who alternated between racing the length of the hallway and zooming back to bark a hello to each person who joined them on the top floor. By the time Florence appeared, sweaty and wheezing, the two larger dogs had sunk to the floor in joyful exhaustion, leaving Ares as the canine welcoming committee. Mammon swiped her tongue across his forehead, spurring him to a fresh round of frenzied spinning before he flopped onto his back and exposed his glossy, tan belly.

"What do we do if she's not in her room?" Florence asked between labored breaths.

"We keep looking until we find her." Jason sounded like a trailer for an action movie.

"What if she's dead?" Eric inquired.

"We freshen our drinks," Dottie said.

"Hear, hear," Castor seconded Dottie's habitual solution to every problem.

"I'm more inclined to follow the maid's example of hiding in my room," Cate said.

"Even if we find her in her room dead?" Rebecca offered a thin smile.

"There's the optimism this weekend needed. Good work, Becky."

"Which room is hers?" Maddie asked, hoping to put an end to the bickering (but not really expecting to get one).

"She should be the second door on the left, between Timothy and Chef Barbara," Carlisle informed them.

"And right across the hall from Maddie, Carlisle and me." Rebecca looked at the assembled group. "Is anyone else noticing a theme?"

"Carlisle and I assigned the rooms based upon a number of factors," Dottie explained. "And I assure you, net worth was not one of our considerations. Now, someone go knock on the door."

Jason obliged with a tap so unexpectedly soft that Maddie, who stood directly to his left, barely heard it. She couldn't help but wonder what reason he had for holding back—perhaps he knew more about Leslie's absence than he wanted anyone to know.

"What good are muscles if you don't use them?" Cate shoved him aside and knocked exactly twice, the sharp crack of her knuckles against solid oak calling the dogs to her side, ready for action.

"Maid?" she called.

"She has a name, you know," Rebecca chided.

"You mean her parents didn't preordain her career path with a prescient moniker?" She sneered and haughtily turned away from a seething Rebecca. "*Leslie*, if you haven't been murdered, open the door." Frowning, she knocked twice more. "Leslie?"

The only response was the sound of Archer snuffling vigorously at the carpet just outside the maid's door.

"She's not in there."

"Or she really is dead. Jason, break down the door," Florence commanded.

"Perhaps we could try simply opening the door before we add destruction of property to the long list of this weekend's tribulations?" Dottie offered.

No sooner had she finished speaking than the doorknob disappeared in Jason's Brobdingnagian hand, but despite the considerable force of his efforts, it didn't budge.

"Now can we break down the door?" Florence asked.

"Absolutely not. Carlisle, the key if you please."

"I left the master key in my room." Carlisle patted down the length of her dress with its entire lack of pockets. "I'll be just a moment."

She hastened toward the other end of the long hallway, her swift movement attracting the dogs' keen interest. Archer, Mammon, and Ares fell in step beside Carlisle, and as the mismatched quartet scampered down the hall, a clearly impatient Florence rapped insistently on the maid's door.

"Let us in," Eric bellowed over the racket of Florence's continuous knocking.

"That'll put her at ease. I'm sure she'll open the door any second," Castor scoffed.

Rebecca spared a second to glare at him before joining the frontlines at the maid's door. "Leslie, we're here to help. At least some of us are." She glowered at Castor once more.

"You think more noise is what this situation calls for, Becky? I see no reason to add to the pointless yelling."

"This can't be happening," Carlisle groaned.

Maddie turned at the sound of her distressed voice. The dogs scrambled to keep up with a now sprinting Carlisle, and though her furrowed brow and trembling hands clearly conveyed her dismay, the dogs remained blissfully unaware of her anguish, focused as they were on the joy of trotting back down the hall.

"Did you find Leslie?" Jason asked.

"Or her body?" Castor said.

"I couldn't find anything. I'm afraid I've been locked out of my room." She looked to Dottie briefly. "I apologize, Ms. Hunter. I never should have allowed this to happen."

"So, you don't have the key?" Eric asked.

Rebecca rolled her eyes. "I doubt she phased through the locked door to get it, Eric."

"That means one of us must have the key." Jason looked equal parts proud of his deductive reasoning and distraught over the follow-up deduction necessary to determine who among them might be in possession of the key.

"Why would someone take the key and lock your door?" Maddie asked.

"To throw us off?" Eric suggested.

"Throw us off of what?" Maddie asked. "Did whoever took the key anticipate a search for the maid?"

"Only if they've been paying attention," Cate grumbled.

Though Cate had a point, what would be the purpose of such a diversion? Maddie doubted the killer would care enough to sow confusion, and at this point, what difference would it make if they found the maid's body or not? They already had three corpses and no idea who the murderer was. One more body would hardly be a concern for the killer. Which meant that the killer likely wasn't responsible for this latest calamity, but Maddie had a good idea of just who the key-thieving culprit might be.

"Why would someone lock Carlisle and the maid's door? Are any other doors locked?"

At Florence's question, Rebecca sprang to action. She dashed to her room but got no farther than the locked door. Undeterred, she moved to the next door, which was Maddie's, and tried the handle to no avail. Still not discouraged, she attempted to open both Chef Barbara's and Timothy's doors, both without success.

"What do we do now?" Florence looked around nervously. "Have all of the bedrooms in the mansion been locked? Is the murderer trying to prevent us from hiding in our rooms?"

Castor turned her way, a look of pure disdain on his face. "Calm down, Flo. Even if we can't get into our rooms, this island is full of places to hide."

"Most of which we can't get to because of the storm," Jason pointed out.

"Thank god we still have access to the alcohol," Dottie said.

"The maid is missing, presumably murdered, but in order to find out we have to get through a locked door without a key. What we need now is a miracle, not a martini," Florence snapped.

"Same thing if it's well prepared," Dottie stated matter-of-factly.

"What if the maid took the key?" Maddie tried to steer the conversation away from another pointless tangent.

"And then locked herself in her room before she was killed," Eric proclaimed proudly.

Castor clapped him on the shoulder. "It's a good thing you're rich, Dillingham, or you'd have nothing going for you."

"The first order of business is getting in the maid's room," Maddie explained. "Once we know if she's alive, we can worry about finding the keys."

"How do you suggest we get in the maid's locked room without a key?" Cate asked. "Gwendolyn already said she didn't want to start destroying property."

The group looked to Dottie, who managed to look elegantly aggrieved. "Fine. Let's break down the door. My chances of recouping my deposit probably died with Helen anyway."

Out of nowhere, a blood-curdling yell pierced the air. Maddie's head snapped in the direction of the sound in time to see a red-faced Eric running straight for the maid's door. What inspired this unexpected act of virility was, more than likely, the woman standing beside her, holding Mammon's collar. Rebecca shook her head in disbelief, and her mouth dropped open (much like everyone else's) as she watched the clamorous, perspiring billionaire charging the maid's door at an impressive speed.

"You're going to hurt yourself." Jason held his large hands up in a warning that Eric chose to ignore, instead barreling ahead on his literal crash course with the door. The rest of the group stood silently by, dumbstruck by Eric's show of intrepidity.

To no one's surprise, the solid oak door didn't budge. Instead, Eric bounced off it like a Superball. His warrior cry transformed into a confused yowl of pain as he stumbled backward, arms flailing wildly. Maddie felt pain blossoming below her eye as his left fist met her cheek. She managed to keep a grip on Archer's collar despite her agony, but she was beginning to wonder if perhaps Carlisle had a point about her aptitude for injury. She hadn't even confronted anyone, and she still ended up with a black eye.

"Are you all right?" Rebecca released her hold on Mammon and turned to Maddie.

"Nothing a good masseuse can't fix," Eric moaned from his supine position on the floor. He gripped his shoulder and grimaced.

"I wasn't talking to you." Rebecca laid a gentle hand on Maddie's cheek. "We should get you some ice."

"I could use some too," Eric whined.

Jason shook his head and stared at the fragile man sprawled on the floral runner. "I told you you were going to hurt yourself."

"I would have been fine if you hadn't distracted me," he huffed.

"Come on, man, you wouldn't even have been fine if you had done it the right way," Jason said. As if to prove his point, he turned toward the door and with one powerful, well-placed kick beside the doorknob, burst through the door and into the maid's empty room.

"She's not in here," he announced.

Whether they needed to see for themselves or they simply didn't trust anyone at this point, the rest of them slowly filtered into the room and searched (with varying degrees of interest) for the missing maid. Florence looked in the closet before joining a reclining Cate on the bed, under which Castor seemed to think he might find Leslie. Dottie inspected the balcony with Jason's help while Carlisle wrung her hands in the corner. Meanwhile, Rebecca held onto Maddie, who cradled her aching cheek and dreaded what would happen next.

"What now?" Eric asked from the doorway. "Does Jason break down every door in the mansion until we find her?"

"There is another master key," Carlisle said. "Perhaps the culprit took that one, and my key is still in my room."

"Who had that?"

"Timothy."

"If I were looking to steal a key, I'd rather raid a spinster's nightstand than a dead butler's pockets." Castor recoiled at Carlisle's schoolmarm stare. "Just saying."

"Castor is right." Maddie shrugged an apology to Carlisle. "Whoever has the key probably didn't take it from Timothy's pockets, which means we're headed back to the wine cellar."

CHAPTER ELEVEN

"Who's going to do the honors?" Castor asked.

They stood in a haphazard semicircle on the periphery of the world's creepiest wine cellar, their collective discomfort palpable. Most of them avoided looking at the bodies, instead taking great interest in the ceiling, the brickwork of which was admittedly impressive. None of them dared to get any closer to any of the corpses, but Maddie noticed that Castor stood as far from them as possible in the increasingly crowded space. At least he wasn't perusing the wine.

Unlike her squeamish counterparts, Cate kept her eye on the pool of blood on the floor and its proximity to her shoes and said, "Shouldn't our resident detective be the one to retrieve the key? After all, she's the one who suggested it."

"I thought we didn't trust her." Eric alternated between rubbing his aching shoulder and scratching his head in confusion.

"I'm not sure we should trust anyone who willingly raids a dead butler's pockets," Florence said.

"It's not like it's a hobby of mine," Maddie replied.

"If it keeps me from touching blood and corpses, she has all my faith." Cate smiled disingenuously and inched farther from the distasteful bodily fluids that imperiled her shoes.

"Thanks for that vote of confidence," Maddie said as thunder rumbled above them, a gratuitous reminder of the raging storm.

Resigning herself to the unsavory task at hand, she squared her shoulders and forced herself to move toward Timothy's temporary resting place. She had no illusions that this would be easy—in fact, she could think of exactly nothing less appealing to her in the moment than rummaging through a dead man's pockets, but if it got her closer to finding the killer and never having to touch a corpse again, she could do it.

"I need more than avoiding an undesirable task to inspire my trust." Florence interrupted her progress. "Maybe you could empty the contents of his pockets onto the table so we can all see it."

"And turn his pockets inside out," Castor added.

"Any other requests?" she grumbled and resumed her plodding progress toward the body.

Gathering her courage, she wiped her hands on the apron she still wore and glanced around at the faces that ranged from open hostility to quiet encouragement. Rebecca offered a thumbs-up while Cate scowled in her direction.

"Be careful, pigeon. Try not to get any blood on the dress."

She suppressed an eye roll, and after a deep breath, plunged her hand into the front right pocket of Timothy's pants, coming up with a comb, a lighter and half a roll of Tums. In the opposite pocket she found two cough drops and fifty-one cents in change, but no key.

"Try his jacket pockets," Jason suggested unnecessarily.

"I really hope it's not in an inner pocket," she muttered as she rifled through the side pockets of his jacket, thankful that, one, he didn't carry a handkerchief, and two, that said nonexistent hankie hadn't been used. She was close to giving up hope when she reached into the breast pocket and there, among some bits of jerky (that she hoped were for the dogs) and a tube of ChapStick, she found the key.

"Aha!" she shouted triumphantly. Her hand shot high in the air before she remembered the solemnity of the circumstances.

"Great. Let's get out of here," Eric cried. He was already halfway to the stairs.

Though she was no less eager to leave the wine cellar, Maddie allowed the others to go before her (not that she had much say in the matter). While Eric and Florence tripped over each other in their haste to put some distance between them and the East Coast's finest corpse collection, Cate and Castor each managed to refrain from running, but not by much.

As Maddie followed Carlisle up the stairs, she paused to look back at the gruesome scene. Of all the things she'd expected this weekend, the hunt for a serial murderer was not on her list. She felt a twinge of sadness for the victims' loved ones. Unless they, too, had pushy rich friends who foisted catastrophic weekend getaways on them, they were probably enjoying their Saturday nights with no inkling of the terrible news headed their way. Though it would be small consolation, she intended to make sure that whoever was responsible faced the consequences.

Maddie emerged from the wine cellar to find Dottie at the kitchen island, holding a pitcher of martinis (thankfully, without a straw). Somehow, in the almost imperceptible span of time that she'd been in the kitchen, she had managed to revivify cocktail hour. Though her robust appreciation for alcohol was, at times, alarming, it was almost comforting to know that not even a triple homicide could throw Dottie's priorities out of alignment.

"Where should we look for our missing maid?" Eric asked. He held a single ice cube in a sandwich bag against his shoulder. Maddie (whose swollen face had begun to throb) couldn't decide whether to be more impressed that he'd found both the ice and a bag to put it in or irritated that he hadn't offered any relief for her.

"Must we begin the maid hunt immediately, or is there time to fortify ourselves for the search?" Dottie took a hearty swallow of her drink as lightning flashed in the rain-battered windows behind her.

"There is some urgency in the matter," Carlisle said. Nevertheless, she distributed drinks to the assembled party. Perhaps she, too, had realized the futility of trying to rush Dottie and her friends.

"The island doesn't lack for hiding places," Castor pointed out.

"Let's assume she's sensible enough not to risk dying in a monsoon just to avoid being murdered."

As if to prove Maddie's point, the wind kicked up, and sideways rain pelted the windows. Rather than abating, the storm seemed to be gaining in strength.

"Can we also assume she's here on the first floor?" Florence asked hopefully. She shifted her weight from one foot to the other.

"That might be overly optimistic since we've mostly been on this floor all night and haven't seen her." Maddie almost hated to crush the woman's hopes of avoiding the stairs.

"There are at least half a dozen rooms on this floor that we haven't set foot in. How can you be sure she's not in the ballroom or the library?"

Maddie turned to Dottie. "Why didn't you tell me there's a library?"

"I didn't whisk you away from your sad, dull existence to let you bury your nose in a book."

"Because that would have been a much worse way to spend my time."

"Pardon me for trying to introduce a little culture to your life."

"Shouldn't we at least check the rooms on this floor?" Florence pressed.

"Yes. What if she's in the billiards room just itching for a game of snooker?" Castor joked.

"Do we need the key to get into any of these rooms?" Maddie asked.

"We have the key, so what's the problem?"

"With only one key and a mansion the size of the Louvre to search, it could take us until Memorial Day to finish."

"You want us to split up?" Cate seemed unduly aggrieved by the thought.

"It is a more efficient plan," Carlisle interjected.

"It would help us find her faster," Maddie agreed, though she'd actually been thinking that searching rooms that didn't lock was a giant waste of time. If Leslie was in hiding, she would choose a room with a locking door, especially if, as Maddie suspected, she was the one who'd pilfered Carlisle's key.

"The last time we split up, I found a body," Florence reminded them.

"And I had to spend time in the stables." Dottie shuddered. "We've all had to endure hardships."

"The way this weekend is going, you might find a body even if we all stick together," Jason pointed out.

"Has anyone seen Ares?" Castor interrupted. His voice conveyed a level of concern Maddie hadn't thought possible for him.

"Or any of the dogs?" Rebecca asked.

"Sorry, no," Cate said, though she didn't sound even a little sorry about the current shortage of drool and dog hair that had compromised her apparel.

Maddie, however, felt terrible since it had been her idea to exclude the dogs from the wine cellar. She'd felt guilty about leaving them behind, but she couldn't justify allowing them inside. There simply was no good reason for them to be there. Though Mammon and Archer, the world's least watchful watch dogs, seemed unfazed by Timothy's death, she didn't think revisiting his corpse would contribute to their continued good spirits. And even if they weren't at risk of renewed depression, the chance that they wouldn't disrupt the scene or tamper with any evidence was too great. So she'd left them whimpering on the other side of the closed wine cellar door, her heart breaking at the chorus of dejection muffled only partially by the barrier between them. Given their great distress at being separated from the pack, Maddie expected to find the dogs wallowing in their misery right where she'd left them.

However, that was not the case. Rather than eagerly greeting each human who returned from the mysterious depths of the wine cellar, Mammon, Archer and Ares were conspicuously absent from the kitchen.

"Maybe they found the maid," Florence offered hopefully.

"I think they found something better," Maddie groaned, realizing the mistake she'd made. She dashed from the kitchen, followed closely by the au courant thorns in her never-fashionable side.

Upon entering the dining room, she stopped abruptly at the sight of massive Archer standing atop the table amidst the fine china and crystal glassware, chomping on the last of the Spam puffs. He'd upended three wineglasses and the thankfully unlit candelabra on his unsanctioned tour of their meal, but every plate was clean. Meanwhile, Mammon and Ares grazed on anything that they could access on the serving cart. Mammon, looking out for the smaller dog, dropped morsels on the floor for her companion, who thanked her with hearty tail wags.

"At least we still have dessert," Maddie muttered and looked to Dottie, who was in full swoon at the complete downfall of her elegant meal. Meanwhile, Carlisle calmly removed the most egregious offender from the forbidden territory of the dining room table.

The dogs looked not the least bit guilty about their unauthorized meal. Archer stretched and yawned, his giant pink tongue unfurling like a party favor before settling at Maddie's feet. His sister belched indelicately and parked herself beside Castor, who cradled Ares in his arms, ineffectively chastising him with baby talk. Mammon pawed at Castor's leg and looked up at the tiny dog, who quivered at a particularly loud clap of thunder but seemed otherwise content.

"We should get back to looking for the maid," Jason said.

"Please don't make me go back up all those stairs," Florence sighed, and sank heavily into a chair that was blessedly free of both crumbs and dog slobber. "I'm not cut out for so much activity, especially in evening wear."

"Aren't you worried about—"

"The only thing I'm worried about is my aching feet."

Another thunderclap rumbled overhead, rattling the glassware on the sideboard. It was as if the house offered no protection at all, and before the rumbling died away, a flash of lightning cracked the sky open, illuminating the grounds as if it were daytime. They stood in silent, terrified awe for a moment until the lights flickered and then went out.

Maddie couldn't tell if the subsequent shriek came from Florence or Eric, but it spurred the rest of them into unfortunate panic. Ares yipped incessantly while Archer howled and pressed against Maddie's leg. Someone shuffled past her, bumped into a chair and swore, and above that noise, she heard toenails clicking against the hardwood floor as Mammon paced nearby, whining.

"Helen is cursing me from beyond, I know it," Dottie griped.

"Does anyone have a flashlight?" Rebecca asked.

"I wouldn't have thought you'd be afraid of the dark, Becky."

"I just want to see your face when I deck you."

A small circle of light flared as the ever-resourceful Carlisle struck a match to light the formerly decorative candles.

"Castor," Maddie sighed, half wishing the next lightning bolt would take him out. "Do you know if your sister had a standby generator? Or why it hasn't kicked on yet?"

"Yes, to your first question. No idea to the second."

"Maybe it didn't like Helen either," Cate offered.

"We need to try to get it running."

"You can fix a generator?" Rebecca seemed pleasantly surprised.

"Not in that outfit she can't," Dottie objected. "I won't have you getting generator muck on couture."

"You'd rather sit around in the dark?"

"It's bespoke," Dottie said, as if that justified taking up residence in a blackout. "Besides, not everything that happens in the dark is bad." She looked to Jason over the rim of her martini glass.

"I hate to kill the entirely inappropriate mood, but aren't we supposed to be finding the maid?" Rebecca asked.

Maddie held back the tormented groan that was desperate to escape. Why couldn't anything be easy? She could have been at home with her dogs and a book and her comfortable loneliness, but instead she was trapped on Assassination Island in a typhoon and had to find a way to restore power and locate the missing maid, preferably before anyone else died. She glared at Dottie. "You're right. This weekend is doing wonders to reduce my stress."

"I'll take a look at the generator," Jason volunteered.

"I'm sure all it needs is a half nelson and it will be good to go," Castor said.

"I was going to use my background in mechanical engineering, but if all else fails, at least I have a backup plan," he said and then flashed his movie star smile.

"And once you've got that generator thing under control, we can start looking for the maid," Eric said.

"We need to find Leslie and fast," Maddie insisted.

"I am not traipsing all over this house by candlelight." Florence was adamant.

"Weren't you the one who was concerned that she'd been murdered?"

"We all were."

Voices rose in anger around her, and until that moment, Maddie hadn't realized how much more out of control a situation could become. She was tempted to go search for Leslie herself but thought the others might notice if she slipped away with the candles.

Just then, a sharp whistle pierced the air. Carlisle glared at each of them, her stern expression made more severe by the flickering candlelight.

"This is the plan. Jason, you'll go fix the generator. Rebecca can help you. Take the flashlight from the kitchen. Matilda will search upstairs for the maid."

"Alone?" Cate objected.

"Of course not. Ms. Hunter and I will accompany her."

"That's not much better," Cate said.

"Fine," Carlisle said through clenched teeth. "You can join us, Ms. Bennet." Castor cleared his throat pointedly. "As can Mr. Andreas."

"And what are Eric and I supposed to do?" Florence asked.

"I could go with Rebecca. Help hold the flashlight." Eric smiled across the room at the unfortunate object of his affections.

"That would be bad for your injured shoulder. You'll help Florence search the first floor."

"But—" he sputtered.

"Excellent. We'll all meet back in the lounge when our assignments are finished. Any questions?"

"None I'm brave enough to ask," Maddie said under her breath.

CHAPTER TWELVE

Maddie was, perhaps, more excited than she should have been at the prospect of searching for Leslie, not because she had a long unfulfilled desire to wander through a darkened mansion on the hunt for a frightened but hopefully still alive maid, but because that search was the perfect opportunity to look for clues in her suspects' rooms. She felt a little guilty about her deceitful multitasking, but she could hardly ignore such a golden opportunity simply because it might be a little insensitive.

That she was also intentionally misleading her pool of suspects just to get a surreptitious peek at their private spaces was probably undoing any good karma points she'd accumulated, but since it was a duplicitous means to a potentially punitive end, she figured she most likely wasn't reserving a seat on the express train to hell. True, she could be more forthcoming about her suspicions that Leslie had taken Carlisle's key and hidden, likely locking the other doors as a way to slow the killer's murderous pursuit of the last service professional on the island.

If she presumed correctly, they wouldn't find their missing maid hiding out in any of the guests' rooms—that would be like a fly choosing a spider's web as the perfect place for a nap. It was more likely Leslie would be hiding in the last place the killer would think to look, namely in one of the victims' rooms. But Maddie, eager to find some link to the killer and hopeful that discovery would take place en route to Leslie's hideaway, kept that theory to herself.

Also true, there was no guarantee that the killer had left a vital clue sitting out for her to find, but what kind of amateur detective would she be if she didn't at least look? It would probably be her one shot to pry, and she wanted to make the most of it. If only Jason would hurry with the generator, she might be able to see the clues she hoped the killer had been foolish (or cocky) enough to leave out in the open. Something like a signed confession would be nice.

While she was grateful for the serendipitous free pass into the suspects' rooms, even if it included two overbearing chaperones, she wasn't loving the investigation by candlelight. Ideally, she would have been alone on this adventure (or, if she had to have backup, with Dottie, who would be so preoccupied with concern over her failed weekend adventure that she wouldn't even pay attention to what Maddie was doing). But of course she had to have an entire cabal of investigators along for the ride and ready to intervene should she stumble upon any useful information. If ever there was an endorsement for keeping to oneself, it was the enforced socializing of this weekend.

Their plodding journey to the second floor was hindered somewhat by the inherent danger of ascending a sweeping staircase in the near total darkness. As she followed the flickering light from Carlisle's candelabra, Maddie wondered how much she resembled the cover of a Nancy Drew mystery. Cate and Castor, on the other hand, devoted their mental energies to such important debates as the proper gin to tonic ratio, the merits of cufflinks versus studs and tie tacks or tie bars. Tensions were clearly high, and though Maddie supposed that disputes over frivolous accessories were preferable to an increased body count, she still did her best to tune them out and focus on the task at hand.

It took an eternity, but they eventually came to a stop in front of the last door at the end of the hall—the master suite Dottie shared with Jason.

"If you're suggesting that I had something to do with the maid's disappearance, we're going to have to discuss severance packages." Dottie seemed none too pleased with her assistant.

"Wouldn't you choose the most well-appointed room to hide in? Not only is it spacious and comfortable, but it also has an attached bathroom. If she had the forethought to bring snacks, Leslie could conceivably stay in there for days. As hiding places go, it's an ideal spot."

"How does it rank on your list of places to dump a body?" Castor earned a glare from his hostess.

"Not as high as the wine cellar," Carlisle answered matter-of-factly.

"By all means then." Dottie gestured grandly at the door, her reluctant permission granted. She still looked like the words "pink slip" were rolling around in her head, but she seemed to agree that her assistant might have a point.

Inside the room, Maddie had to stick close to Carlisle, keeper of the candelabra, to get a good look at anything, and unfortunately, she hadn't intuited Maddie's ulterior motives. Thus, she moved swiftly around the perimeter of the room, pausing briefly at the bulky, ornate dresser, the rain-soaked French doors to the balcony and the four-poster bed, where Cate made a show of lifting the bed skirt and calling, "Maid, come out." They didn't come to a complete stop until they reached the closet. The dogs, having vigorously sniffed a swath across the hardwood floor, sat at eager attention, apparently enthralled by women's finery.

As Maddie rummaged through the flotilla of dresses testing the tensile strength of the hanging rod, Dottie snapped, "Must you manhandle every garment? Do you think Leslie has constructed a designer fort?" She paused her apparel abuse long enough to spare an exasperated sigh. "Careful with the Valentino, pet."

Maddie made a show of delicately shifting the dress she guessed was the fragile item in question and continued her sartorial journey to the far end of the closet, where she found exactly two suits squeezed between Dottie's fashion armada and the wall. Below them sat an impossibly small leather duffel bag, dwarfed by Dottie's Louis Vuitton luggage set. Why the woman needed two rolling suitcases, a carry-on, a garment bag and a cosmetics case for a weekend trip was beyond Maddie's comprehension. Not even someone as fashion-forward as Dottie could conceivably wear all of these clothes in three days' time, especially considering the number of hours she devoted to her beauty rest.

Maddie, enshrouded in tulle and satin and still determined to find answers to the mysterious murders plaguing their weekend, crouched down to open Jason's bag, but the meager light disappeared as Carlisle moved toward the fireplace, leaving Maddie no choice but to follow. The area in front of the fireplace had a couch, chairs, and a coffee table. It seemed to Maddie like an odd place for entertaining guests, but then again, everything about this weekend had been odd. The fireplace itself was large and ornate, and above it, a blanket hung precariously. As decorative elements went, it was fairly incongruous.

"What's this?" she asked, pointing to the dark cloth.

"A slender barrier between me and a nightmare."

Dottie removed the blanket, revealing yet another portrait of Helen, this one somehow less flattering than the others. The artist had depicted a field of wrinkles on the landscape of Helen's face, like a freshly plowed pasture of dissatisfaction. Her downturned mouth and cold, stern eyes seemed to cast judgment on the entire room. It was a brazenly unattractive portrayal of its subject, one that left Maddie with the impression that the artist had enjoyed working with Helen about as much as one would enjoy preparing for a colonoscopy every other day of the year.

"I wanted it removed, but Carlisle had no luck taking it down. Because of course, Helen would bolt a portrait of herself to her bedroom wall, even if it is deeply disturbing."

"And it's still more flattering than the four she rejected." Castor glowered at his sister's image.

"I hope the artist got hazard pay," Cate said.

While the group was distracted by Helen's perplexing display of vanity, Maddie slipped a candle from Carlisle's candelabra and stole away to the bathroom. Her immediate impression was that the room was being consumed by cosmetics. It was like a Sephora exploded. If she had hoped to find anything to incriminate or exonerate Jason, she would have to wade through a gallon of Crème de la Mer and enough eyeshadow to cover the cast of a Broadway musical. As far as she could tell, Jason wasn't even allowed to use the bathroom (or he had exquisite taste in moisturizers).

The wire wastebasket beside the vanity had been filled to capacity with cosmetic-covered cotton balls, lipstick-blotted tissues, and farther down, what appeared to be blood-soaked tissues. Maddie recoiled at the thought of inspecting it further. She didn't care if it provided the details of each murder plus incontrovertible evidence against the killer. She was not about to rummage through Dottie's biohazard trashcan. She excused her investigative shortcomings with the innumerable possible explanations for the blood—Jason could have gotten a bloody nose or cut himself shaving, or it could be from when he cut himself the night before. She supposed it could be Dottie's blood (though considering its alcohol content, it was more likely that her blood would evaporate before reaching the tissue), or it might even be from Timothy or Chef Barbara. As clues went, it was fairly inconclusive.

Opposite the trashcan sat a hamper overflowing with dirty clothes. She had no idea how Dottie had managed to produce so much laundry in just over twenty-four hours, even with Jason's assistance. The obvious explanation was that Dottie was a fashion overachiever, but another possibility was that Jason had experienced some unexpected wardrobe changes after bumping off three people. Though the odds of finding any useful information were low and the ick factor was high (but not as high as the wastebasket), she would be remiss if she didn't at least check the hamper for clues. What if Jason had deposited a bloody shirt in there?

"I'm happy to see you're taking an interest in a beauty regimen, Swiss roll, but this is hardly an appropriate time. The lighting is not conducive."

"I'm looking for clues," she whispered, her hand still poised above the hamper.

"Look no more, Judas. I assure you that you'll find nothing. Jason is not our murderer."

"I need something more than your word on the matter, especially since you can't provide an alibi for him for last night."

"I would know if I was sleeping with a murderer." Dottie arched an eyebrow and crossed her arms.

"I guess we'll find out," Maddie muttered and reluctantly followed Dottie from the suite and down the hall to the next stop on their servant scavenger hunt. Not that she trusted her thrice-divorced friend to be an excellent judge of male character. She simply didn't want to draw unnecessary attention to her covert detecting by arguing about Jason's murderous potential.

When they arrived at Cate's door, she tried to prevent them from entering. "No maid here," she declared after a half-second peek from the doorway.

"We can't even see the bed from here," Maddie pointed out.

"I seriously doubt she's silently cowering beneath the duvet."

"Let's just make sure." Maddie pushed past her, followed by the rest of the search party, and immediately tripped over an open suitcase in the middle of the floor. Its contents were strewn everywhere, almost as if the room had been decorated by wind. The nightstand overflowed with crumpled tissue and lipstick-smeared glasses, and on the bed, a mound of cast-off clothing sat atop a tangle of sheets.

"It's safe to say the maid has not been anywhere near this room," Castor said.

"How did you do this much damage since yesterday?" Maddie was almost thankful for the poor lighting that prevented her from getting a better view of the alarmingly messy state of Cate's room.

"Good of you to leave room for Leslie to hide in your closet." Dottie deftly navigated the couture minefield of Cate's floor, grimacing as she went.

"I'm a very busy woman. I don't have time to clean."

As Maddie tried to get her bearings in the disaster area, Ares trotted past with what appeared to be a pair of white granny panties, which he dropped at Castor's feet like an offering.

"This room is full of surprises." He smirked and held the sturdy undergarments aloft for all to see.

Cate struggled to retrieve her underpants from Castor, who kept them just out of her reach, and Dottie looked on in horror as her urbane weekend devolved into an uncouth game of undie keep-away. Meanwhile, Maddie used the distraction as an opportunity to peruse the disarray of Cate's closet.

Somehow she'd found the resolve to hang up two of her dresses, but that had been the extent of her strenuous unpacking. She'd carpeted the floor with dirty clothes (that she was now trying to shoo the dogs away from), and her precious shoes—so susceptible to the dangers of grass and rain—had been tossed carelessly in a heap. Maddie supposed she should be impressed that they had at least been corralled in a designated shoe pile. Nothing in the room pointed to Cate as the killer, though to be fair, she could have a bloody murder weapon in there and Maddie would never find it in the mess. So far, it appeared that slovenliness was Cate's only crime.

"You really put the filth in filthy rich," Castor teased.

Carlisle stood in front of him, hand extended, and he forfeited the underpants without argument. He was unnecessarily cruel at times, but he did have a point—in spite of her put-together appearance, Cate was kind of a slob, which meant she probably had used every second of the time between the search for Timothy and cocktail hour to achieve her deceptively polished look. It wasn't an iron-clad alibi, but it did make Maddie reconsider the likelihood that she was the guilty party.

"I believe we've established that the maid isn't hiding in here." Cate scowled at her tormentor. "Perhaps we should move on."

"Of course," Maddie agreed, hoping to find something of investigative value in the next room.

If Cate's room was a tribute to slovenly living, Eric's was a surprising homage to tidiness. And horses. The bed had been made (with a decorative horse pillow thrown in the superabundant bedding mix), and on the bedside table sat a horseshoe key ring as well as a hoof pick. The latter seemed like a strange item to bring to an island entirely devoid of horses, but perhaps Eric was an eternal equestrian optimist. In his closet she found a small collection of shirts with a decidedly equine theme, all neatly pressed and hung tidily.

"This is a man who knows how to organize." Carlisle beamed at the sight of the shirts, slacks and jackets hanging at quarter-inch intervals. She cast a brief judgmental glance at Cate and then returned her gaze to the organizational wonder that was Eric Dillingham's temporary closet. "He's even brought a tie rack." Carlisle admired the apparently vital tool that (thank god) kept unsightly wrinkles at bay.

"I know I'm impressed," Maddie muttered and moved to Eric's dresser.

Atop the dresser, he'd neatly arranged his brush, a horse-emblazoned bottle of Pegasus Exclusif cologne and a beard comb. Alongside those treasures were two framed photographs.

"He travels with pictures of his horses?" Maddie asked no one in particular as she tilted the eight by ten frame toward the candlelight to get a better look. She doubted the glossy headshot of Apollo would in any way link Eric to the murders, yet she couldn't help her curiosity. Given his extreme fascination with all things equine, Eric seemed superficially harmless, like a seventh-grade girl but with a bigger budget and marginally better taste.

She set the photo back in its place on the dresser and started opening drawers, all as neatly arranged as his closet. Just as she was about to close the drawer on the visual of Eric in his horsey boxer shorts that was now seared into her mind, Castor's hand closed around her wrist.

"Is Leslie the Incredible Shrinking Woman? Or a contortionist, perhaps?"

"It wasn't on her résumé," Carlisle answered matter-of-factly.

"Then we probably don't need to look for her in a drawer."

"Right you are," Maddie said and backed away from Castor.

"Can we leave this room yet?" Cate asked. "God, it even smells like horses."

"I don't believe you're in a position to discuss the state of anyone else's room," Dottie said.

"Had I known I was responsible for providing my own maid service this weekend, there wouldn't be an issue."

"Yes, many people are afflicted with the inability to properly use a hanger without a maid present."

Cate huffed angrily and stomped out the door, and as Maddie followed in her wake, she began to wonder if she was wasting her time. Perhaps the killer was too calculating to leave clues behind, and all of her snooping would amount to nothing. Meanwhile, she was putting Leslie's well-being at risk. If she hadn't already been killed, the poor woman's extended tour of duty in fear of that event would surely set her up for a hearty dose of PTSD down the line. But there was no way to change course now without revealing her secret spy mission. Unless she wanted to invite the wrath of Castor and Cate upon her, there was nothing to do but press forward and hope for an investigational miracle.

Castor's room was almost disappointingly mundane. Though he wasn't particularly organized, he was infinitely tidier than Cate (a claim that could be made by most humans over the age of three). Ares had scattered several of his toys across the floor, almost as if he was easily distracted, and as soon as he grew bored with his plush dinosaur or his squeaky peapod (with detachable peas), he dropped it and moved on to a crinkly rope whale or a bunch of plastic grapes. There was no shortage of dog toys for Ares to choose from, and in fact, he had more toys to himself than Maddie's boys had between them. For all of Castor's maddening qualities, at least he loved his dog.

And thankfully, dog toys were the only tripping hazard in Castor's room. His clothes were put away and his luggage was stowed in a corner of the closet. Equal parts curious and hopeful that she could justify their protracted search, Maddie pulled the zipper on the suitcase, but before she got the bag open, Cate stood over her, clucking her tongue.

"First Eric's drawers, now Castor's luggage. How small do you think the maid is?"

"Well, I'm in the market for a new suitcase, and this one caught my eye. Such craftsmanship." She stroked the bag appreciatively while Cate frowned her disapproval, inspiring Maddie to continue her search elsewhere.

Ares's monogrammed dog bed sat a few feet away from the fireplace. His blanket (also monogrammed) was pushed to one side, revealing a small cache of even more toys and other curiosities—a Kong, a silk scarf that surely didn't belong to him, a stuffed squirrel, a chintz throw pillow, two Nylabones and a squeaky tennis ball that brought all three dogs to Maddie's side when she squeezed it. Ares immediately jumped in his bed, barked at Maddie and pulled the blanket over his toys like a protective barrier.

Leaving Ares to his horde, she turned to the fireplace, which had been used recently. It occurred to her that none of the other guests had put their fireplaces to use. It seemed odd that Castor would. True, the weather had been crisp the night before, but she doubted it was cold enough for someone as shiftless as Castor to go through all the effort of building a fire when there were blankets nearby.

"I'm surprised you lit a fire," she verbalized her thoughts.

"What can I say? I tend to run cold."

"Like a reptile," Cate said.

"Or your marriage. Remind us, where is my ex-brother-in-law this weekend?"

"He's on a business trip. Unlike some people, he actually works."

"For your sake, I hope it's not the same kind of work that led to his divorce from Helen."

Cate charged across the room, but before she reached the still smirking Castor, Dottie intervened.

"Unless this contretemps is somehow going to help us pinpoint the maid's whereabouts, I suggest you focus your energies elsewhere." Dottie scowled at her guests, who did as they were told, with Castor peeking behind the curtains while Cate checked behind the door for their truant maid.

Clearly reaching the limits of her patience, Dottie sighed, drained her glass and glided out the door, compelling the search party to move on to the next room.

Walking into Florence's room was almost like stepping onto a blank canvas—there were so few personal touches here that the space seemed unused. The bed was made, and other than a heating pad on the nightstand, Florence had left no personal effects out to be seen. The room was completely anonymous aside from the closet, which they gathered before, staring at its bland contents: a smattering of dresses in various shades of gray and brown, three pairs of dress shoes (all flats) and her sturdy, plain suitcase.

"Her wardrobe is as dull as she is," Cate said. "Why anyone thinks brown is an attractive color is beyond me."

"All she does is work and take care of her mother, so unless you're hoping to find an elderly Latina woman lurking behind the matronly dresses, you're probably going to be disappointed."

"Florence has a great deal to offer," Dottie roared, "though fashion sense isn't one of those things."

Maddie drifted over to the dresser, not really expecting to find anything of value, and for once she wasn't disappointed. Florence seemed to excel at drab.

Even the dogs seemed bored. They'd curled up at the threshold and drifted off to sleep. By unspoken agreement, the search party exited Florence's antiseptic quarters and continued on their pilgrimage.

"We're checking Helen's room?" Castor seemed startled as Carlisle opened the door to the room where his sister had stayed on the last night of her life.

"It's not like she'll object," Cate said, pushing past him. Whether she was curious to invade Helen's privacy or eager to end this search, Maddie wasn't sure.

Considering how little time Helen had spent in the guest room assigned to her, it wasn't surprising how little they found. Helen had tossed a business suit on the unused bed. Maddie assumed it was the outfit she'd traveled in as she hadn't seen it before. Castor, in an uncharacteristically reflective moment, touched the sleeve of his dead twin's jacket, running his fingers over the material with something close to affection.

The only other indications that Helen had even entered the room were her locked suitcase (at which the dogs sniffed energetically) plus her laptop and a partially consumed glass of scotch on the nightstand. Maddie eyed the laptop. She'd love to see what secrets it contained, but with her eagle-eye wardens close at hand, she doubted she'd even get it open before the lambasting began. But what were the odds that she could sneak it out of the room with no one noticing? And if she pulled that off, then what? Hide it under her dress until they found Leslie? That seemed impractical at best, and considering that it was Helen's laptop, she would probably need not just a password, but fingerprints, a retinal scan and three drops of a virgin's blood to access any information, meaning that, even if Maddie pulled off her improbable heist, it would all be for nothing.

"Leave it to Helen to waste perfectly good alcohol." Dottie sniffed at the glass and set it back where she found it.

"My sister always did have more money than sense," Castor offered wistfully before seeking comfort from Ares and exiting the room.

"Why don't we move to the third floor?" Carlisle suggested delicately. "I'll lock up behind us and meet you at the stairs."

Carlisle joined them at the second-floor landing just as the sound of labored breathing came floating up from somewhere below. The small search party froze, watching as flickering candlelight inched its way up the stairs and the wheezing increased in volume.

"If I die on a staircase, I'm going to haunt you all," Cate announced and scooted to the rear of the group.

"If that's the killer, we can rule out the element of surprise." Castor sounded less like his impish self than usual, and Maddie wondered if that was due to fear or residual melancholy from the scene in Helen's room.

"Aren't you guys finished yet?" Eric called from the landing below. He'd paused there, presumably waiting for the even slower-moving Florence to catch up. "We expected you back ages ago."

"I thought we'd be done ages ago too," Cate sighed. "How much more time are we going to invest in this little endeavor?"

"You have somewhere else to be?" Dottie asked.

"What happened to you not wanting to traipse all over the mansion in the dark?" Maddie asked Florence.

"Eric took all the candles." Florence glared at her search buddy's back.

"I offered to leave you one."

"So I could sort of see the killer coming to get me? No, thanks." She leaned against the wall to catch her breath. "What's left to search? Please don't say the third floor." Florence sank a little lower in defeat when everyone else avoided eye contact with her. "Fine. Let's go. But my next vacation is going to be somewhere without stairs."

The lackluster efforts of the second-floor search were outstanding compared to the group's exertion once they reached Rebecca's room. Florence and Cate sat on the bed and watched as Castor strolled aimlessly around the room, holding Ares in one arm and picking up random objects with his free hand—a currently pointless cell phone, a half-empty glass of water and the latest installment in a mystery series about a crime-solving real estate agent in Phoenix.

Across the room, Dottie gasped at the open closet. "My god, she's an indigent."

Maddie glanced inside the closet, finding jeans, dress pants, several casual and dressy tops and not a single dress. Essentially, it was what Maddie's closet would have been if she'd had any control over her wardrobe. But thanks to Dottie's pastime of using Maddie as a living paper doll, her closet was overrun with admittedly beautiful but completely out of character gowns instead of being a haven for slacks like Rebecca's.

"You mean she didn't pack like a pioneer gearing up for a cross-country migration? The nerve."

"I find your insouciance as bewildering as this ghastly wardrobe."

To Maddie's eyes, it was more a source of envy than horrified indignation. "It's almost like she doesn't know that it's a crime for women to wear pants."

"Have no fear. I'll set her straight, so to speak."

"Is it okay to be going through her things like this?" Eric faltered in the doorway, clearly as uncomfortable as he was ineffectual. At least he wasn't using this as an opportunity to sniff Rebecca's underwear. He might be a weak-chinned, semicontemptible murder suspect, but at least he wasn't a creep.

"Apparently privacy means nothing when the maid has gone missing," Castor muttered and made a show of peering behind a potted plant in the corner.

Rolling her eyes and reminding herself of her hidden agenda, Maddie turned her attention to the bedside table, almost dreading what she would find, not that she objected to discovering the truth about the killer. She just hoped that the truth wouldn't point to Rebecca. And unless the key to solving this mystery lay in a hairbrush or a contact case, then Rebecca was still in the clear, and Maddie was no closer to finding the killer.

Beyond verifying Leslie's absence, Maddie saw no reason to explore Carlisle's room. She almost certainly wasn't the killer, but even if she had managed to bump off three people in under twenty-four hours while still tending to Dottie's every whim, there was simply no way she would be sloppy enough to leave any clues behind. Nevertheless, despite Maddie's desire to bring this futile endeavor to a close, the rest of the group barreled ahead, fully prepared to repeat their cursory examination of improbable hideouts such as beneath the pillows or behind the obligatory portrait of Helen. If their desultory attempts to locate the maid hadn't distracted them from Maddie's simultaneous (and ultimately pointless) hunt for clues, she might have found it more irritating.

It felt a little strange walking into Carlisle's room, like she was reading her diary or eavesdropping on a private conversation. A very dry conversation about alphabetizing and the benefits of packing cubes, which Carlisle had in abundance. She also had the most expansive collection of sweater sets in the continental United States, all neatly folded and arranged in her drawers according to their position on the color wheel. Of course, the bed had been made, its soft flannel sheets pulled taut enough to bounce a roll of quarters to the twelve-foot ceiling.

"Did you bring your own sheets?" Maddie asked, amazed at the depths of Carlisle's ultra-preparedness.

"I shipped them in advance with the rest of my things."

"How efficient," Eric observed, much to Carlisle's delight.

Maddie turned away from the Efficiency Appreciation Society and scanned the rest of the room. The closet held three Dottie-approved party dresses as well as several boxes with preprinted shipping labels. On one end of the dresser, Carlisle had laid out her jewelry: a silver necklace adorned with a crossed arrows pendant, a matching bracelet and clip-on earrings, all at precisely spaced intervals. The rest of the dresser top was reserved for Carlisle's extensive Dottie-care essentials: an iPad, charging cables, her ever-present clipboard and a handheld steamer (because Dottie's wardrobe, like her skin, was a wrinkle-free zone).

As Maddie suspected, there was nothing here—or anywhere in the mansion—to help her case. In just under an hour of searching for Leslie and any clues to the killer, the only thing Maddie had discovered was that she wasn't much of a detective, a realization that was surprisingly disheartening. It wasn't like she dreamed of solving murders or that she longed to put herself in danger. That's why she (like everyone else present) had initially resisted Dottie's suggestion that she embrace her inner gumshoe and capture the killer among them. But now, a whole day into her investigation with nothing to show for it and no idea what to do next, she felt inexplicably saddened by the probability that this weekend would signal the end of her crime-solving days.

Resigned to the notion that her covert sleuthing would amount to nothing, she decided to bring it to an end. While Carlisle was busy debating the best label makers with Eric, Maddie slipped the master key from the assistant's pocket.

Amazed that she hadn't been subjected to a choke hold or otherwise subdued, she hurriedly crossed the hall from Carlisle's room and stood wearily in front of Timothy's door. She felt certain (or as certain as a failed amateur detective could feel) that they'd find Leslie either here or in Chef Barbara's room, and taking a gamble, she unlocked Timothy's door, prepared to be disappointed yet again.

The door opened with a creaking groan, and Maddie strained to see beyond the flickering glow of her candlelight. She took a step forward and felt a whoosh of wind followed by the thump of a down pillow hitting her face and knocking her backward. She dropped the key but had no time to retrieve it before another thwack from the pillow sent her reeling again. Her butt hit the floor just as the candle flew from her hand, tumbling end over end and extinguishing before thudding against the floor. While a small part of Maddie's brain was relieved not to set fire to the mansion, that minor consolation was eclipsed by the awareness that she was now trapped in the dark with the Babe Ruth of bedding.

A flash of lightning illuminated the hallway long enough for Maddie to see her assailant winding up for another blow. She threw her hands up defensively and braced for the impact. Leslie screamed and swung again, but the ever-resourceful Carlisle appeared from nowhere and once again substantiated Maddie's ninja librarian theory. Using the handle of her unused umbrella, she hooked Leslie's leg and yanked, sending the maid and her surprisingly effective weapon tumbling to the floor.

And with the perfect timing typical of her life, the lights came back on, and Maddie looked up to see the entire search party gathered around her, drinking in her latest humiliation.

"Good news," she offered from her position on the floor, "I found the maid."

CHAPTER THIRTEEN

At Dottie's insistence, they gathered in the lounge for post-search cocktails to settle their nerves. As one of only two people who'd been in any real danger, Maddie gladly accepted a drink (if not the flimsy excuse for it). In truth, she was more interested in talking to Leslie before she got spooked into hiding again. Ideally that conversation would have happened in private, but of course, everything about this weekend had been the antithesis of ideal.

Before they'd all made their way to the lounge, Castor poured ten brandies then drained and refilled his glass. Leslie's hands shook as she sipped her drink, glancing nervously around the room at her supposed heroes. After some prodding, she apologized for stealing the key from Carlisle's room and causing so much commotion.

"Why were you hiding?" Eric asked.

"Did you miss the memo about the killer on the loose?" Rebecca snapped.

"But why would the maid need to hide? And why in the butler's room? Is this a servant thing?" Eric prodded.

"Two thirds of the victims certainly were." Castor's comment elicited a glower from Carlisle, but he merely shrugged and poured himself another brandy.

"I figured that the killer would want to keep me quiet about what I've seen."

"What did you see?" Almost everyone asked the question in unison. Dottie, however, was too preoccupied with the pursuit of stronger spirits to be invested in the maid's recent tribulations.

"Nothing. But the killer doesn't know that, and I didn't want to end up in the wine cellar like the others. I hoped the killer wouldn't think to look in Timothy's room since he's already—" Tears welled in her eyes, and she gulped her brandy while they waited for her to collect herself. "When I heard footsteps in the hall, I thought for sure I was done for, so I grabbed something to defend myself with. I'm awfully sorry about that, miss."

She turned her teary, apologetic eyes on Maddie, who waved off the offense. "I'm just glad Timothy didn't keep any hammers in his room."

"I do feel safer now that I'm not alone." Her tremulous voice and terrified eyes belied her claim.

"Even though one of us is a murderer?" Eric asked.

"Why would you point that out?" Rebecca hissed.

"You just said the same thing a minute ago."

"The point," Maddie interrupted, "is that even though we still don't know who the killer is, we're safer in a group."

"That's terrific, but we'll need to sleep at some point," Cate said. "How do you propose we handle the sleeping arrangements if we're all sticking together?" She looked from Eric to Castor and shuddered.

"The ballroom is large enough for all of us. We could sleep in there, maybe move some of the couches or the mattresses—"

"And then what?" Dottie asked. "Play Light as a Feather, Stiff as a Board? This isn't a slumber party, and I refuse to bunk down on the floor like I'm in a halfway house. We'll sleep in our beds as Stearns and Foster intended."

"And what if we're killed in our beds?" Florence argued.

"At least we'll be comfortable before we go," Dottie quipped. "Besides, I believe we've established that the doors all lock. I'd advise you to take advantage of that fact."

"That's your solution? We just lock our doors and hope that the murderer is feeling lazy?"

"It worked for Leslie."

Maddie didn't share Dottie's confidence in the security of a locked door. Among other things, Jason had already broken down one door, and there was no reason to believe he couldn't do it again. If he was the killer, a locked door wouldn't necessarily stop him. True, the rest of them would hear the commotion, and even if they didn't come running at the sound of wood splintering, they'd see the damage and have a good idea who was responsible. So, unless Jason was a fool, he probably wouldn't break down any doors in an effort to try to hide his murderous secrets. The killer had been cunning and brutal thus far and wouldn't likely make such an obvious announcement of his or her identity when they were so close to getting away with it. Maddie took little comfort in that thought, however.

They debated the sleeping arrangements for another thirty minutes but ultimately decided that turning a lock would be simpler than moving furniture from the second and third floors. Maddie didn't necessarily feel safer locked in her room, but at least Mammon and Archer had followed her to bed. Not that they offered much protection from anything other than a good night's rest, unless of course the cacophony of canine snoring was a natural murderer repellent.

As if to prove her questionable worth as a guard dog, Mammon stretched expansively before rolling over and thumping Archer's nose with her massive front paw. Her brother grumbled in his sleep but didn't bother opening his eyes. Clearly, the threat of fatigue outweighed the imminent danger of the executioner in their midst.

Considering the savage nature of the deaths, Maddie didn't share in their tranquility. After all, they were talking about an ax murderer who also dabbled in bludgeoning and strangulation, hardly a circumstance conducive to sound sleep. Even less comforting was the likelihood that the killer would get away with it if she didn't find some answers soon.

As she wrestled with her thoughts, she watched the shadows dancing across the ceiling of her room while the trees outside her window shook and swayed in the wind. They intermittently tossed precipitation against the panes, though the rain had subsided almost an hour earlier, about the same time she'd given up hope of ever falling asleep. She shifted uncomfortably and tried to sit up in bed, but the snoring hundred-pound dog sprawled across her midsection prevented her from doing much more than craning her neck to look around the room. When Archer rolled over and snorted, she availed herself of the increased mobility and sat up, rubbing her eyes.

"At least someone can sleep," she muttered, and glanced at the clock.

She'd lain awake for close to two hours, her racing mind as tempestuous as the weather as she replayed the unexpected turn of events in the past twenty-four hours. That morning, her biggest concern had been how to talk Dottie out of whatever fashion nightmare she had in store, not how she would solve a triple homicide in two days' time. Given the option, she'd happily exchange her current predicament for the opportunity to wallflower her way through another cocktail party in the designer fashion of Dottie's choosing, heels included.

But instead of embracing the alternating mortification and obscurity that was life as Dottie's sidekick, she was busy nursing her insomnia with worries about how many bodies they would find in the morning and scrutiny of their conversation with Leslie. Who knew that navigating the periphery of an awkward social engagement in avant-garde frippery would be the pinnacle of her weekend?

"If only I had something to go on," she grumbled. "How am I supposed to catch a killer when I don't have any clues?"

The dogs slept through the question and her subsequent realization that she *did* have a clue—the weird pin she'd found in the wine cellar earlier. She'd meant to show it to Dottie, but as the day had gone from bad to horrific, she'd forgotten all about it.

"I have to talk to Dottie." She leapt from the bed, grabbed her toiletries bag and raced from her room.

As she crept down the hall toward the stairs, the floor creaked beneath her, and she froze, hoping no one had been roused by the noise. Over the sound of her pounding heart, she heard the clamor of toenails clicking against the hardwood floor. Mammon and Archer trotted up behind her, wagging their tails vigorously, obviously delighted at taking part in another exploit. She considered banishing them to her room as this mission required a certain amount of stealth, which had thus far not proven to be one of their strengths. But she thought better of it when she considered the possibility of encountering someone in the hallway. The dogs offered both an easy excuse for wandering from her room and at least the hint of protection should she need it.

"But you have to be quiet," she whispered and held her finger to her lips, immediately feeling ridiculous for doing so.

Her anxiety mounted when Archer mistook the universal signal for "quiet" as a command to howl. Not to be outdone, Mammon began spinning excitedly in a circle, the thudding of her enormous paws during her frenzied gyrations adding to the clamor that was sure to get them caught.

"Yes, that's exactly what I meant," she groaned and grabbed Mammon's collar, bringing an end to her twirling.

Archer coughed out one more tiny howl that trailed off in a yawn before looking up at Maddie expectantly, as if he should be rewarded for alerting the entire household to her furtive nighttime activities. She supposed she should thank him for not racing up and down the halls and barking at each closed door. Aware that was a distinct possibility, she took hold of his collar as well and braced herself for the repercussions of her prowling.

After a tense minute during which no one opened their doors, Maddie released her hold on the dogs and continued down the hall. Chances were good that Dottie was still awake, though what state she would be in after her millionth martini was another question entirely. Considering the abundance of alcohol she'd consumed, she might have passed out hours ago. Or, Dottie being Dottie, she might be mainlining vermouth at that very moment. But since time was in short supply, she had to take the chance that Dottie would be both awake and useful.

Halfway down the hall, she stopped suddenly, bringing an abrupt end to the stentorian pilgrimage of her immense furry shadows. How was she supposed to consult Dottie on the only clue to this mystery when she was sharing a bed with one of the suspects? She couldn't exactly ask Jason to wait in the hall while she discussed his possible murderous tendencies with his girlfriend. Not only would she upset her friend by banishing her paramour from the room, but it might also alert the killer to her minimal progress. If Jason opted to tell the others that she'd made some headway, the guilty party might decide to add her body to the wine cellar's holdings. Unless Jason was the killer and decided to take care of the problem then and there.

But when would she have another opportunity to employ Dottie's specific skillset without the prying eyes and ears of everyone on the island? Her personal wardens, Castor and Cate, weren't likely to stand idly by while she snuck off for some secret sleuthing, and she already knew the futility of investigation as a group activity. It wasn't an ideal situation, but the risk of letting Jason in on her find was preferable to sharing her potential breakthrough with her entire pool of suspects.

As she passed the last room before the staircase, the door opened, a hand flew out and grabbed Maddie by the arm, eliciting a startled yelp from her as well as three sharp barks from her attendants. She was pulled inside the room, and as she struggled to free herself, her bag fell just inside the door. She looked to the dogs for help, but they merely darted through the open door. So much for their alleged protection. Once the door closed behind her, the grip on her arm released, and she spun around to see a flannel nightgown-clad Carlisle smirking at her.

"What are you doing? Are you trying to give me a heart attack?" she snapped, inciting more barks from the dogs.

Carlisle's raised-eyebrow glare quieted their barking and sent them scurrying to her bed for comfort. She offered them a frown and a headshake before turning her attention back to Maddie, who couldn't help but appreciate Carlisle's obvious frustration with the recalcitrant hounds.

"Must you be so dramatic, milkweed? You'll wake the others."

"I'm sorry. I'll try to control myself the next time I'm abducted in the midst of hunting for a brutal killer." Dottie stifled a yawn as she retied the belt on her silken robe. Her obvious readiness for bed raised several questions. "Why are you in Carlisle's room? Shouldn't you be working on your standard twelve hours of sleep?"

"Normally, beauty rest is paramount in my world, but grisly murder has taken momentary precedence. We need to find the guilty party and fast. Before my name becomes synonymous with ax murdering." Dottie fell back on Carlisle's bed, jostling the dogs who had made themselves comfortable there. "By now, I imagine you need my wise counsel, hence your nocturnal perambulations."

"Maybe I just wanted to stretch my legs."

"While our resident assassin is still at large? I don't think even you are that foolhardy. Besides, this is how we solve murders. You scout for clues, and I piece them together for you."

In hopes of staying somewhat on track, Maddie ignored that piece of revisionist history. "That still doesn't explain why you were lying in wait in Carlisle's room."

"I knew you wouldn't want Jason to be privy to the details of the case, so I told him I needed to confer with Carlisle regarding the revised agenda for tomorrow. That business having been attended to, all that remained was biding our time until you appeared on the scene, and voilà here you are."

"Sorry to keep you waiting." Maddie was amazed that Dottie had acknowledged, even inadvertently, Jason's possible hand in the murders. She still hoped that her best friend hadn't been sleeping with a killer but finding that out for certain would be far simpler if she didn't have to combat Dottie's willful delusions along the way.

"Not to worry, pet. We've had a most productive meeting, and Carlisle even has a special surprise for you." Dottie nodded at her assistant, who opened the bottom drawer of her dresser and retrieved a laptop. Not just any laptop—Helen's laptop.

"Perhaps this will help your investigation."

"What? When did this happen? How did you get Helen's computer?" Maddie sputtered.

"I saw you eyeing it during our search for Leslie, so before I locked Helen's room, I appropriated it. It was easy enough to stow it in my drawer while everyone else was fixated on my closet."

"I don't suppose you found all the answers we need on it?"

"I'm afraid I didn't do more than figure out the password before Ms. Hunter appeared at my door."

Speechless, Maddie sank on the bed beside Mammon and opened the laptop. She had no idea what to expect—perhaps it held the secret to Helen's murder or possibly it would be a colossal waste of time. Regardless, she was hardly in a position to reject a lead, no matter how slim it might be.

"You can invade Helen's privacy later, jellyfish. Tell us where you're at with the case before I retire for the evening."

"Not very far, I'm afraid. This is all I've got." She retrieved her toiletries bag from the floor where she'd dropped it in her surprise.

"I'm all in for renovating your look, but this is hardly the time."

"My look is fine," she grumbled, and dug for the pin.

"Let's not oversell it, raisin bread." Dottie took the pin from Maddie and examined it closely, her expression appreciative. "Where did you find this?"

"Beside Helen's body. What is it?"

"It's the mark of superior taste. Obviously, it didn't belong to that termagant."

"Could you elaborate?"

"It's Isaia."

"Thanks. That clears everything up."

"Would it kill you to learn just the tiniest bit about fashion?"

"Then what would you have to disparage me for?"

"I'd find something, buttercup. When the fashion door closes, the gods of cosmetology open a window."

"Something to look forward to," Maddie grumbled. "Care to enlighten me?" Dottie gasped in obvious delight. "Keep it brief."

"Fine. Isaia is a clothier of the highest order—clean lines, classic elegance, everything a gentleman could want in a suit. And this pin"—she held up the item in question—"adorns every suit jacket, distinguishing the wearer as an individual of great discernment."

"And since the pin most likely came from the murderer, you're saying that we can identify our killer if we know who wore this designer last night?"

"Fashion doesn't seem so frivolous now, does it?"

Maddie couldn't believe it was that simple. She'd been struggling for hours to find something, anything to go on, when she'd had the answer all along. She didn't know whether to rejoice that the killer would pay for his crimes, to mourn the loss of so many hours of her day or to brace for Dottie's redoubled efforts to school her in the world of fashion.

"Do you remember who wore what last night?"

"Let's see." She rose and paced the floor, her forefinger on her chin as she cast her memory to the previous night's sartorial offerings. Maddie watched her friend's expression fluctuate as she contemplated the apparently difficult question of her guests' ensembles. "Cate was dazzling in that alluring silver gown. And the cut—A-line does wonders for her. Still, you could have outshone her, you know."

"Maybe next time."

The gleam in Dottie's eyes told Maddie she would live to regret that statement.

"Where were we?"

"You were salivating over clothing."

"Not over Florence's. She opted to adorn herself with a bland number from the uninspired collection. I preferred Rebecca's trousers, and you know how I feel about women's pants as evening wear."

"This is all very enlightening, but aren't we looking for a man?"

"Respect my process, kitten."

Maddie fell back on the bed, resigned to an unnecessary inventory of every guest's wardrobe choices. She supposed she should be grateful not to have a replay of what everyone travelled to the island in.

"If it helps, you can skip the replay of the servants' ensembles."

"If you continue to interrupt me, I'll begin enumerating accessories."

Dottie spared her a withering glance and resumed her pacing. She covered the length of the room one and a half times before she blanched and sank onto the increasingly crowded bed with Maddie and the dogs.

"It can't be."

"What?" Maddie tried to keep the impatience from her voice. Dottie, however, remained exasperatingly silent.

"If memory serves," Carlisle took over for her employer, who was in full swoon, "Mr. Van Dam was wearing Isaia."

"But it couldn't be Jason."

"You can't will him into innocence, Dottie. The man is violent for a living."

"He's a performer, not a brute killer. And he's not the only one we should be looking at. Remember Castor's dashing purple jacket?"

Maddie had noticed the article in question. She didn't know too many men who wore purple. "Let me guess—same designer?"

"So you see? Jason isn't guilty," Dottie announced triumphantly.

"That's hardly a rock-solid alibi," Maddie pointed out to Dottie's great displeasure. "It has to be either him or Castor."

In spite of the unexpected ambiguity of her only clue, Maddie felt buoyed by this development. After all, her pool of suspects just shrank by two thirds.

"Not necessarily." Carlisle shattered that burst of optimism.

Maddie whimpered in her frustration, briefly rousing the dogs. "You're telling me that Eric also wore this designer? Did they get a group discount or something?"

"Of course not. Eric is strictly a Corneliani man."

"That doesn't leave a lot of options."

"There are still two other possibilities." Maddie stared at Carlisle, awaiting an explanation. "When Florence returned from her walk, she was chilled, and Castor loaned her his jacket. She would have had an opportunity to take his pin. This was, of course, after her argument with Helen."

"Of course, the one time Castor thinks of someone other than himself, it thwarts my progress." Maddie groaned in exasperation and then gasped as memory dawned on her. "Rebecca had a pin on her jacket. There's no way—"

"Unfortunately, there is," Carlisle coolly confirmed Maddie's fear.

It seemed like any time she came close to finding answers, something got in the way. But this was the closest she'd gotten to finding the killer, and it was the only solid clue she had to follow. It might not lead her directly to the killer, but she had to pursue it.

"Maybe that won't matter," she said. She hoped for a simple explanation, disappointing though it might be to Dottie. "We need to see whose pin is missing."

"Mr. Andreas isn't likely to let you back in his room."

"What if we don't need his permission?" Dottie smiled devilishly.

"What are you thinking, Dottie?"

"I'm thinking it's the perfect time for a fashion show."

"Isn't that sort of like asking the people of Pompeii to model their tunics while Mt. Vesuvius is erupting?"

"You need to get a look at the guests' habiliments, and we need an activity to fill the hours tomorrow. I had originally intended another repast, but this is so much better than crude dining and the looming threat of Monopoly with Eric."

"Won't it seem odd if you ask people to rewear their outfits? Especially since so many of them packed for an eternity rather than a weekend?"

"I can be most persuasive where Castor is concerned, and he's our real quarry."

"Even though we still have several other suspects, including Jason?"

"Cupcake, I have access to Jason's wardrobe."

And a blind spot the size of Jupiter, Maddie thought.

"A fashion show seems a bit much. Can't you just distract Castor while I sneak into his room?"

"Starfish, if you haven't noticed, almost everyone is on high alert regarding your investigation. Even if Castor isn't watching you, someone else likely is, and they might find it suspicious if you wander into his room while he's otherwise occupied."

"But no one will think twice about an impromptu fashion show?"

"They might find it surprising, but why would they ever suspect it's a ruse to catch the killer? Whereas you rummaging through Castor's wardrobe is sure to raise suspicion."

Maddie opened and closed her mouth a few times to object, but she had to admit that Dottie had a point. A fashion show was somehow both more and less inconspicuous than trying her hand at breaking and entering. And if Dottie couldn't manipulate her guests into an unwitting parade of alibis, she could always resort to her original plan.

"Can you organize a fashion show in less than a day?" she asked, still hoping to rein in Dottie's tendency toward excess.

"You wound me. I've thrown together far more intricate affairs with far less notice, and with Carlisle's help, it will be a breeze." For her part, Carlisle seemed mildly aggrieved about the most recent addition to her duties.

"Then I guess I'm about to see my first fashion show."

"Kitten, you won't be watching. You'll be participating."

"How will I spot the culprit if I'm busy parading around in front of everyone."

"If you're observing rather than participating, then the jig is up. They'll know immediately that we're up to something."

"Or that I'm fashion averse."

"Trust me, tartlet. This is the only way the plan will work. Besides, I already know exactly what you're going to wear." The devilish gleam returned to Dottie's eye.

"Terrific," Maddie sighed, wondering how likely she was to catch the killer before her runway debut.

When Dottie dismissed her twenty minutes later, she left the room feeling cautiously optimistic—not about her chances of avoiding further humiliation, but that Dottie's absurd idea might just work. True, it would do little more than eliminate a suspect (possibly two), but at this point she would take any progress that came her way.

Her tempered good spirits lasted only until she passed the open door to Timothy's room. She was certain that door, like all the others, had been closed on her initial pass, and though she hadn't checked, she felt confident that it must have been locked as well. After all, why would Leslie, who had been so terrified of the killer earlier that she'd locked every bedroom door in the mansion, now neglect to even close the door to the room where she was spending the night? It made no sense. Regardless, she knew it couldn't mean anything good.

She looked to the dogs, who seemed to share her trepidation. Mammon issued a low growl at the door, and Archer whimpered and shifted nervously. In spite of every instinct screaming at her not to do so, Maddie knocked on the door and softly called out for the young maid. The eerie silence that surrounded her did little to quell her nerves. "I have the dogs with me. Don't hit us with a pillow," she added as an afterthought.

Still hearing nothing, she reassured herself that she was probably safe. How likely was it that the killer was hunkered down in the maid's room as part of some elaborate plot to eliminate her and her investigation? Unless the killer was a mime, the chances of his or her complete silence seemed improbable. Still, her first act after nudging the door completely open was to flip the light switch, so at least she'd see her attacker before being struck down.

Instead, she saw Leslie, motionless on the bed, her face covered by a pillow.

"Maybe that's just how she sleeps," Maddie said to the dogs.

As a group, they inched closer. With every shuffling step, the knot in Maddie's stomach grew larger. She studied Leslie's body, trying to discern the steady rise and fall of her chest with her breaths. None came. She reached out to touch Leslie's shoulder, and still the woman didn't move. Finally, Maddie removed the pillow from the young woman's face only to have her worst fears confirmed.

While she conferred with Dottie and Carlisle just a few yards away, the killer had committed another bold and terrible murder.

CHAPTER FOURTEEN

"How could I let this happen?" Maddie sank to the floor in disbelief.

The only sound in the room was the deep breathing of two exasperated dogs as they settled on either side of her. Time stretched as she sat there absentmindedly stroking Mammon and Archer and staring at Leslie's lifeless body. She knew she should move. She should tell someone about what had happened, or at the very least, she should leave the scene of the latest crime, especially since the killer was still at large and not even slightly deterred by her efforts to catch him. But no matter how much she told herself to go, she couldn't seem to make her body listen to her brain, so there she sat.

This was her fault. Not entirely, of course. She hadn't held a pillow over Leslie's face as she struggled for air, but Maddie also hadn't prevented the killer from striking again. More damning, she realized now, she'd dropped Timothy's key when Leslie first hit her, but she'd never picked it up. The killer must have taken advantage of the confusion in that moment. And then, rather than insisting that they stick together, Maddie had just let Leslie go off to her death alone. No matter how she looked at the situation, she couldn't absolve herself from blame. All she could do now was redouble her efforts to catch the killer, preferably *before* she found another body. But with less than thirty-six hours, very little in the way of evidence and a ridiculous, sure-to-fail plan in her corner, she couldn't help wondering what her chances were.

And as if Dottie's incredibly flawed plan wasn't already a gamble, now Maddie couldn't even be sure that the murderer hadn't overheard them discussing the pin and how best to capitalize on it. She was certain that Leslie's murder had taken place while she was just down the hall conferring with Dottie and Carlisle; however, she simply had no way of knowing what else had transpired while she was distracted by fashion talk. If they were lucky, the culprit didn't take any chances beyond the rather large risk of committing murder in the middle of the night with at least three potential witnesses nearby. But having already gambled with getting caught, perhaps the killer decided to do some snooping of their own. Surely, they could have seen the light under Carlisle's door. It wasn't unreasonable to surmise that curiosity got the better of them and brought them within hearing range of planning for The Great Fashion Show Gambit. If that was the case, she had little hope that their ploy would work. Knowing their ulterior motive in advance would mean that the killer could avoid falling into the trap that was set. And since it was a thoroughly ridiculous trap to begin with, no one would look unreasonable for not wanting to go along with it.

Faced with that possibility, Maddie's inertia worsened. If not for the inherent creepiness of doing so, she would have laid down there between the dogs and waited for this curse of a weekend to be over. But, no matter how hopeless the situation seemed, camping out on a dead woman's floor would accomplish exactly nothing. Maybe she stood no chance of catching the killer, but that didn't mean she should just sit around waiting to be butchered.

She supposed she should tell the others about poor Leslie. Not only did she not know how to hide it from them, she also couldn't forget their anger over the secrecy of Chef Barbara's demise. She dreaded the idea of rousing them from their sleep (assuming anyone had managed to doze off under their current conditions) with news that not only had the killer struck again but now also had an all-access pass to their rooms. Perhaps she should get a second opinion—or better yet, some backup in the form of Dottie's imposing presence. She should at least let Dottie and Carlisle know that they had another body on their hands and that their plan had been compromised. Though she felt a twinge of guilt at the thought, the possible bright side to this horrible situation was that it might make Dottie call off her fashion show. Then again, she might come up with something even more ludicrous instead.

Finally spurring herself to action, Maddie rose, and with her canine cortege in tow, headed back toward Carlisle's room, hopeful that she'd catch Dottie before the commencement of her beauty sleep. She took exactly three steps and collided with a blue chambray wall. Stunned, she shook her head and looked up to see Jason staring at her, his expression amused with a hint of something else—malice? Guilt? Surprise? She couldn't be sure.

"I'm so sorry." She stepped back. "I didn't expect to run into anyone."

"Well, you did a great job of it anyway." He grinned, and for Dottie's sake, she tried to find it more charming than menacing.

"What brings you to the third floor in the middle of the night?" She intended to sound innocently curious but doubted that she pulled it off.

He gestured toward Carlisle's door, his words slow to come. "I came looking for Gwendolyn. She stepped out a while ago, and with all the murders, I was worried about her."

"I'm surprised you let her leave."

"I think you know as well as anyone the challenges of dissuading her." He laughed uncomfortably.

"But you were coming from the other direction."

"Yeah, about that. I figured I might as well check on my sister while I was out and about." He scratched the back of his head nervously. "She hates it when I big brother her."

"If that's anything like being big sistered, I understand her aversion. How is she?"

"Sound asleep, apparently. She didn't answer the door."

"But the door was still locked?" Sudden apprehension knotted her stomach.

"Of course. What's going on? Why are you up?"

Maddie opened her mouth to offer her ready excuse when a low voice from behind Jason cut her off.

"You should know I'm trained in the art of Brazilian Jiu-Jitsu."

She and Jason stared at the door behind him as it creaked open just far enough to reveal a nightgown-clad Carlisle, poised to strike. At the sight of her boss's boyfriend, Carlisle's stance immediately shifted. Maddie wouldn't call it more relaxed, but it was definitely less aggressive.

"I apologize. I heard noise in the hall and thought perhaps it was the killer."

"And your first instinct was to channel the Karate Kid?" Maddie asked.

"I like to face problems directly." She offered a thin smile and turned to address Jason. "Is there something I can help you with?"

"Only if you know where to find Gwendolyn. I'm getting worried about her."

"You dear man." The door flew fully open and Dottie emerged, her robe covering noticeably less of her anatomy than before. "I was just preparing to depart. How gallant of you to check on me. Matilda?" Her head swiveled in Maddie's direction, and she adopted an overdone expression of surprise. "I'm absolutely gobsmacked to find you here."

"Seems I'm catching everyone off guard."

"I would have thought you'd be locked away in your room by now. Why on earth are you wandering about in the dark of night?"

"I was just taking the dogs for a walk." Thankfully, Mammon and Archer didn't contradict her story by retreating to her room or wandering down the hall to savor the aromas present at each doorway.

"With a laptop," Jason said. He gestured toward the computer she'd forgotten she clutched.

"Well, you never know when you'll need to make a spreadsheet."

"Oh god. What happened now?"

This latest interruption of Maddie's abysmal attempts at covert ops came from Rebecca, who stepped into the ever more crowded hallway and stretched. The snug T-shirt she wore rose to reveal a tantalizing glimpse of a flat stomach that Maddie absolutely did not notice. Nor did she distract herself by zeroing in on the well-muscled length of thigh on full display below pale-pink shorts.

"I'll just go take care of the dogs."

"And the laptop," Jason reminded her.

"As you know, I love a good spreadsheet myself." Carlisle seized the computer from Maddie's hands. "Perhaps later we can compare notes." She all but winked, and Maddie wondered if loss of subtlety was a side effect of too much exposure to Dottie.

"Want company?" Rebecca asked, already falling in step beside Maddie.

Maddie absolutely did not want company. She wanted to retreat to her room and figure out what to do about the latest murder and how to prevent further carnage, neither of which could be easily accomplished under Rebecca's watchful eye.

"Sure," she said, and continued toward the stairs under the ruse of concerned canine guardianship.

Outside, the world seemed strangely quiet considering the tumult of the day thus far. An occasional breeze fluttered through the leaves of the trees, carrying with it the lingering scent of rain. Maddie stood on the edge of the lawn, watching the dogs as they carefully sniffed the ground before turning in a few lazy circles and plopping onto the still-damp grass. They clearly had no interest in acting as her cover story, and instead they closed their eyes and resumed the sleep she'd so rudely interrupted. Even so, focusing on them helped her not to dwell on Rebecca's proximity and the surprising beauty of the moon that hung low in the sky and the fact that neither of them was talking, though presumably, that's what Rebecca had intended when she offered herself as company.

Her flannel bunny pajamas and thoroughly unglamorous terry-cloth robe being no match for the chill of the night air, Maddie hugged herself for added warmth. But despite the cold, the dogs' tattletale behavior, the stress of her investigation, the weight of her responsibilities and the burden of Leslie's recent demise, Maddie was in no hurry to rush back inside. For one thing, the peaceful night seemed like a reprieve from Massacre Manor. In there, she had no hope of avoiding multiple deaths and the hunt for the responsible party, but out here, she could gaze at the moon and stars and forget for a moment that people's lives might very well depend on her ability to catch a killer with nothing but a pin and a contrived fashion show to go on.

The other compelling reason to brave the chill of the night stood just a few feet away, rubbing her bare (and arguably swoon-worthy) arms for warmth. Rebecca was wildly underdressed for a moonlight stroll in frigid temperatures, but the less honorable side of Maddie wasn't sorry to have her company in that moment. Rebecca shivered, igniting Maddie's more chivalrous side.

"Here. Put this on." She wrapped Rebecca in her robe, receiving an appreciative smile that staved off the chill for at least another minute.

Reluctantly, Maddie turned away from that inviting face, and by unspoken agreement, they began walking down the path toward the woods surrounding the property. Their leisurely pace contributed to the overall peaceful illusion that Maddie found herself more and more inclined to embrace in spite of the lingering awkward silence and her own internal dialogue surrounding it.

She'd assumed that Rebecca had ulterior motives when she insisted on accompanying her—why else would she brave the cold with the island's least popular living occupant? But perhaps she'd been wrong (an all too common occurrence where Maddie and beautiful women were concerned). Perhaps Rebecca, too, just wanted a reprieve from inherent tension of the mansion. Maddie wondered how long the silence would continue when Rebecca finally spoke.

"You being awake had nothing to do with the dogs, did it?"

"Not exactly." Maddie grimaced. Technically, they had impeded her sleep, but putting the blame entirely on them was like giving full credit for a hangover to that last glass of wine.

"Is it too much to hope that it had something to do with me?"

"I wish it did," she said and for the millionth time that weekend looked around for a rock to crawl under. Thankfully, Rebecca let the comment slide.

"He didn't do it, you know." Rebecca's voice was quiet but still managed to break through Maddie's thoughts.

"What's that?"

"Jason. I know you suspect him, but he didn't do it."

"How do you know?"

"Because I know my brother. You have the wrong idea about him."

"How can you be sure?" Maddie asked, hoping that Rebecca's certainty didn't spring from the fact that she herself was guilty.

"Just trust me. He's not a murderer."

"So Dottie keeps telling me," she muttered.

"On that point she's right." Rebecca favored her with an all-too-familiar look where Dottie was concerned—a quizzical look of amused concern. "He doesn't even kill spiders."

While that was objectively admirable in most circumstances, it hardly equated to proof of innocence. Still, in spite of her better judgment, Maddie found herself hoping that what little evidence she had so far was painting the wrong picture—about Jason and his little sister.

"But you don't know me. You don't know what ideas I have about him."

"So why don't you tell me what you're thinking, and I can tell you all the ways you're wrong."

"I'm not sure that's the best idea. I know you love your brother, but—"

"But what? That doesn't make him innocent? I know that, but I also know he would never do something like this." She gestured behind her at the mansion. "He would never hurt anybody.

"I hope you're right."

"I know I am."

Unsure of what to say, Maddie looked back at the mansion. They'd wandered much farther than she'd realized. She hadn't intended to stay out so long—in fact, she hadn't intended to go out at all, but Rebecca had forced the issue. Now she wondered if there was a hidden agenda. Rebecca's flirtatious behavior did little to quell that concern. If someone like Rebecca was flirting with someone like Maddie, it was probably based more on the circumstances of Maddie's investigation than any possible attraction. No, flirting from Rebecca was not to be trusted.

"We can head back if you want," Rebecca said.

"Is that what you want?" Maddie asked. She didn't know what answer she hoped for.

"You're honestly asking if I have a preference between a walk in the moonlight with you or taking my chances with a killer?"

Maddie turned back toward the house, but Rebecca laid a gentle hand on her arm, stopping her. "I thought my choice was more obvious than that."

She smiled almost shyly and grabbed Maddie's hand. Her eyes fell to Maddie's lips and she stepped closer. With her free hand, she touched Maddie's chin, gently tipping it upward, and then time stopped as Rebecca's soft full lips touched hers. Maddie's breath hitched, and she fell into the kiss. She cradled Rebecca's face, and though they itched to travel elsewhere, she kept them in place, her thumbs gently stroking those magnificent cheekbones. Rebecca's arms tightened around her, and the kiss deepened. Maddie couldn't have stopped the whimper that escaped if she wanted to, but she didn't want to. She only wanted to lose herself in this moment, in this amazing feeling. She wanted to forget about murder and mayhem and absurd fashion shows and the fact that she was making out with a murder suspect's sister. Gasping, she drew back.

"What are you doing?" she asked breathlessly.

"For a detective you're kind of clueless."

"I just mean—if you're planning to seduce me into believing your brother is innocent—"

"I promise only one of us is thinking about my brother right now." She moved to resume the kissing, but Maddie stopped her with a hand on her chest.

"This isn't a good idea."

Rebecca offered a captivating smile. "I think we'll have to agree to disagree about that."

CHAPTER FIFTEEN

Maddie supposed that a solitary early morning run on an island where murder seemed to be a more regular occurrence than the sun rising was the pinnacle of bad decision-making. However, for her it was also a reliable source of mental clarity, something she desperately needed in that moment. Not only did the plague of murders in the last two days still confound her, but now she was also unsettled thanks to her romantic life's recent (and not to be trusted) emergence from hibernation. Both situations, impossible though they seemed, demanded her attention. So as the sun inched its way above the horizon, signaling the start of a new day—the last full day she had to catch a killer—she braved an encounter with the island's resident executioner and headed out for a run.

At first, she moved aimlessly but cautiously around the island. It wasn't like she could get lost, and she had no goal in mind but to allow the fresh air to stimulate her thus far fruitless thinking. She absentmindedly followed the same path she had the day before, a misshapen loop around the perimeter of the property, but when she reached the teahouse, she realized that this was an ideal opportunity to snoop around the scene of Timothy's murder—or at least what the killer had led them to believe was the scene of the murder.

Checking the surrounding area for prying eyes, she moved to the rear entrance. Several downed branches obstructed the path, and as she suspected, the storm had obliterated almost everything that might resemble a clue. Nevertheless, as she scaled and limboed her way to the door, she glanced about for something helpful to her investigation. Aside from sodden leaves and grass, the only noteworthy sight was what appeared to be wheelbarrow tracks. But even if Maddie could be sure that's what they were, she had no way of knowing when they'd appeared. Maybe the killer had used a wheelbarrow to move the body, or maybe Timothy had done some landscaping earlier in the week.

Inside, the scene looked just as she remembered—drag marks and a trail of blood leading to the piano. Obviously the killer had dispatched Timothy elsewhere and relocated the body, but she had surmised as much yesterday. What she didn't know was why, and where had the murder taken place? She might never know the answer to that question but hoped she could solve the murders without that rather significant piece of information.

Careful not to damage any evidence the police might need when they took over the investigation, she crept toward the piano, on the lookout for anything she missed yesterday. But even without the unhelpful input of her pool of suspects, any potential clues or fresh insights eluded her. As she stared at the concert-ready piano, wondering if the murderer had been trying to send a message (and what that message might be) or simply having macabre fun with Timothy's death, she had the nagging feeling that she was missing something obvious. Unfortunately, scrutinizing Timothy's death tableau did little to help her identify what that thing was.

She spent the next twenty minutes covering the ground between the teahouse and the nearby structures before deciding that she was getting the opposite of clarity. Everything about the scene in the teahouse was staged, yet nothing stood out as an answer to any of her questions, no matter how many times she envisioned it, and continuously reflecting on it was rapidly becoming more frustrating than beneficial. It didn't help that her thoughts kept drifting to strong arms and soft lips and a moonlight encounter that was almost too magical to believe.

Back in her room after a shower that did no more than her run had to provide answers, Maddie smiled in spite of herself at Ares, Mammon, and Archer, comfortably lounging on her bed. She wondered what her next move should be. At some point she'd have to let everyone know that the killer had struck again and now also had a key to their rooms. Obviously, she should have done this the night before, but things had gotten more than a little complicated by her encounter with Jason and the subsequent fallout. She was also still reeling from her improbable make-out session with Rebecca. Under normal circumstances "Everyday Maddie" would spend the next several hours obsessing over the kiss and how unlikely it was that she'd attracted the notice of a certifiable knockout like Rebecca. "Murder-Solving Maddie," on the other hand, had no time for such paranoid indulgences.

"She couldn't like me, could she?" she asked the dogs. She paced the room, occasionally glancing at her attentive (if silent) audience. "I mean, you guys have seen her. She's gorgeous." All three dogs wagged their tails in agreement. "And then there's me." She gestured to herself, and the tail wagging intensified. She scowled. "What do you know? You sniff butts willingly."

The dogs' heads snapped to attention at the sound of firm knocking on the door.

"Maybe it's Rebecca. You like her, remember?" she said to them and immediately chastised herself for nurturing optimism.

The moment Maddie opened her door, an oversize garment bag was thrust in her face. She stumbled backward under the weight of it and managed to peek around the bulky item to find Carlisle staring pointedly at the ceiling.

"I don't wish to interrupt anything."

"Except my need for oxygen." She shifted the bag to a moderately less uncomfortable position and waited for the explanation she assumed was forthcoming.

"Ms. Hunter would like you to wear that for the evening's festivities."

Maddie gulped as a fresh wave of dread hit her—nothing that came in that package could be considered a good thing. Meanwhile, Carlisle lingered on the threshold, shifting uncomfortably from one foot to the other. She still hadn't made eye contact.

"Perhaps when you're alone, we can discuss other matters."

"I'm alone now. Unless you think the dogs are acting as double agents."

"You don't have company?" Carlisle's disbelief was palpable.

"Only of the four-legged variety." She gestured to the small menagerie crowding her bed.

"Odd. I thought, perhaps, after your late-night excursion with Mr. Van Dam's sister that you might, um…"

"Forget about the prolific killer on the loose long enough for some sexploits?"

"One never knows."

"I'm not Dottie."

"Pardon me for noticing the attraction."

"Who wouldn't be attracted to Rebecca?"

"I was referring to her attraction to you."

Maddie had no time to recover from that pronouncement before Carlisle's demeanor returned to its standard aloof efficiency as she bustled into the room and extracted Helen's laptop from some hidden fold of her sweater.

"I found little of use, at least as pertains to this case. If I were interested in corporate espionage, or seizing control of a smaller, less powerful company, this would be a treasure trove." She opened the computer and typed in the password. "The one noteworthy item gives Florence an even stronger motive. I know you're leaning toward Mr. Van Dam, but you should take this into consideration."

Maddie squinted at the screen full of legal jargon but failed to make sense of it before Carlisle opened another file containing communication between Helen and Florence. The gist of it seemed to be that Andreas Corp. was facing a significant lawsuit and that Helen expected Florence to "make it go away."

"Shouldn't Helen have had attorneys handling this?"

"And she did. There's substantial communication between her and the legal team regarding this situation. It seems, however, that she was leaving nothing to chance."

"But Florence was hesitating."

"And Helen was prepared not to take no for an answer." Carlisle pointed out another file which contained intelligence on Florence's elderly mother whose status in the country was questionable at best.

"There's no indication that Florence knew what Helen was planning."

"True, she may not have been aware of Helen's machinations, but she had to know that Helen was unhappy with her hesitancy. That plus the threat to her job l—"

"Makes one hell of a motive." Maddie wedged herself on the bed between the dogs, who grumbled at the disruption of their cuddling.

"And she had access to the pin. She could easily be your killer." Carlisle snapped the laptop shut, and with the waters significantly muddied, turned toward the door. She paused before exiting. "I have much to attend to before the event tonight, but if you need further assistance with your investigation or…any other matters, I'm available."

Maddie didn't even have a chance to utter her thanks before the door closed, leaving her alone with the dogs and her thoughts. Not two minutes after Carlisle vanished like fog, another knock sounded. It seemed unlikely that superefficient Carlisle might have forgotten something, but given the absolute absurdity of the weekend, she supposed anything was possible. It was an unexpectedly pleasant surprise to lay eyes on Rebecca dressed in running shorts and a red and white tank top.

"I'm about to hit the gym with Jason. I thought maybe you'd want to join us." She gestured over her shoulder, a clear invitation to hop on the fitness train.

"I'd love to but—"

"But you have a killer to catch, and you think that it might be my brother, so this is a really bad idea. But there's also the part where exercise is proven to increase mental acuity, which is probably helpful in circumstances like this." She offered a sly half-smile. "Plus, I really enjoyed our walk last night, and I thought this would be a good follow up. Because of how it will help clear your head."

"If an early morning run didn't clear my head, how would the gym be any different?"

"First of all, I can't believe you didn't invite me to go running with you. I'm sure I could have done something to help you out."

"I'm suddenly regretting the oversight."

"It's not too late."

Maddie joyfully focused on Rebecca's smile when a thought occurred to her. "You said Jason works out every day?"

"Just about. It's kind of his job to be fit, and moving corpses isn't really enough to keep him in shape."

"No, I don't suppose it would be," she muttered, her mind already racing. "I've been looking at this all wrong."

When they'd needed to move Timothy's body to the wine cellar, Jason had handled the transport all by himself. He'd lifted the dead butler easily and carried him all the way back to the mansion and down the stairs without so much as a complaint or any need to stop and rest. He'd never asked for help or indicated in any way that it was a burden. So why would he have needed to drag Timothy's dead body through the teahouse to the piano? Unless he was trying to throw them off, it simply made no sense for Jason not to carry the body when he was perfectly capable of doing so. She felt extraordinarily feebleminded for her failure to put those rather obvious pieces together. Although, just like everything else about this case, it wasn't irrefutable proof that he was innocent, she still felt like she was inching her way toward the truth and that that truth pointed to a different guilty party.

"Thank you." She planted a grateful kiss on Rebecca's lips and turned to go find Dottie, but a hand on her wrist pulled her back.

"Whatever I did, I think I deserve more thanks than that."

"I'll make it up to you tonight," she said, not even caring about the impression she'd just made.

Maddie's patience had disappeared right around the time the third body had been found, so when she arrived at Dottie's door, she offered a cursory knock and entered without waiting for any acknowledgement. It was only fair considering how frequently Dottie had barged into Maddie's home unannounced.

Inside the suite, she looked around but didn't immediately find Dottie or Carlisle. Assuming they were in the throes of (hopefully superfluous) fashion show planning, she wandered farther into the room, stopping short the moment she beheld Dottie's dizzyingly zigzag patterned derriere undulating in the air roughly two feet above the floor. It shifted and inched forward as its owner crawled along, her hands fumbling around for whatever she was in search of. A few feet away, her assistant conducted a similar (if less chic) exploration.

"What are you doing?" Despite her straightforward question, Maddie braced herself for any number of absurd explanations.

"Thank goodness you've arrived, Matilda." Dottie ceased foraging for only a moment. "This is an all-hands-on-deck situation, so kindly lend us your hands." She pulled Maddie down to the floor beside her and resumed her mystery hunt.

"This would be easier if I had some idea what we're looking for."

"Jason's pin."

"Excuse me?" Maddie reared back, put her hands on her hips and waited for more information.

"Jason's pin is no longer with his suit, so we're searching for it."

"Did you try looking next to any corpses?"

"No, skunk cabbage, I haven't because, unlike you, I haven't convinced myself that he's guilty."

"I never said I was convinced."

"But that's all changed now, I'm sure."

"Actually—"

"The simple fact that he happens to possess a replica of your only clue and now that item has vanished does not mean you can condemn him."

"I don't want to condemn him. That's what I came here to talk about."

"I knew you would succumb to my powers of persuasion eventually."

Maddie's groan of frustration died on her lips as Jason entered the suite unexpectedly. He stopped just a few feet from the door and stared at the three women still kneeling on the floor near the closet.

Dottie rose to greet him. "You're back early."

"I forgot to grab a towel." He cast a glance toward the bathroom, almost as if he expected to find more lurking guests crawling around his room. "What's going on here?"

"We're desperately trying to salvage this weekend."

Jason looked from Dottie to Maddie, as if he expected a more coherent answer from her.

"I just got here a minute ago." Maddie threw her hands up defensively.

"Dottie?"

He looked to their hostess, and Maddie gasped at his use of her nickname. She braced for the apoplectic fit that was sure to follow, but Dottie simply smiled sweetly, took Jason's massive hand in hers and offered not only a reasonable explanation of the scene he'd walked in on but also an impressive attempt to wheedle information from him.

"I had hoped that, tonight, I could see you in the Isaia you wore on Friday. You were so dashing. It would be a shame to keep that look bottled up. I was going to lay it out for you, but the pin is missing. It's just not the same without the pin. Do you know where it might be?"

"I hadn't even realized it was gone." He scratched his head, the muscles of his forearm dancing as he did so. "I guess I could have lost it when I demonstrated the octopus hold for Eric and the others."

"Octopus hold?" Dottie sounded equal parts relieved and horrified.

"Here, let me show you." He moved behind Dottie and hooked a leg around hers.

"What others?" Maddie interrupted the tutorial.

"Castor was there." Jason resumed his previous position but stayed close to Dottie. "Cate showed up too. I guess she'd been trying to call her husband but couldn't get a signal."

"So this was after dinner?"

"That sounds right."

Of course it was. Because what fun would it be if her only clue didn't somehow point to every suspect?

"I guess I might also have lost the pin when we, um, took a walk in the woods."

"Ah yes. That was a vigorous *walk*. So many things could have been lost. Maybe we should take another walk and try to find it."

Dottie and Jason moved even closer to one another, seemingly oblivious to the others in the room, and Maddie suddenly wished teleportation was a part of her skillset. Before the scene in front of her became R-rated, she cleared her throat aggressively. "I hate to interrupt this tender moment, but maybe you should hold off on your walk until after your workout. Rebecca said she was meeting you."

"And she'll push me twice as hard if I keep her waiting." He retrieved his missing towel and made his exit, stopping briefly at the door to wink at Dottie.

As soon as the door closed behind him, Dottie spun in Maddie's direction, relief emanating from her person. "Thank heavens his innocence has been verified."

"I'd hardly consider two questionable possibilities proof of innocence."

"Did you even listen to the man? He was grappling in couture. That could have any number of calamitous results. In truth, his only crime is virility, extreme virility." Dottie's lifted eyebrow and knowing smile held all the subtlety of a flashing neon sign, and Maddie longed to be stricken with a rare case of short-term sensory deprivation.

"Dubious though his explanation might be, now that we're certain Jason's pin is missing, we need to find some other way to figure out who's responsible for all the carnage this weekend."

"You aren't suggesting we abort our plans, are you?"

"A fashion show isn't going to help us now."

"Au contraire. It could be most beneficial."

"Because wasting time looking at outfits will somehow help me solve this case?"

"Duckpin. Fashion is never a waste of time. And we can't know for certain that Castor hasn't also lost his pin. We need to verify."

"How likely is it that both of them lost their pin?"

"How likely is it that one third of us would be slain in two days' time?"

"Even if both of them managed to lose their pins on the same night, that's not going to help me. It just makes my only clue even less helpful."

"But Castor doesn't know that we know that the pin is missing, so if we confront him about it, we can still have our answers."

"You don't think he could lie?"

"He most assuredly would. He's a manipulative weasel. Lying is like oxygen to him."

"So then how does a fashion show help?" Maddie wanted to pull her own hair out.

"Among other things, it gives my guests something to look forward to other than their own grisly demise. I can't offer them a fine dining experience. There's no one to prepare, serve or clean up. Any chance of good conversation faded when suspicious accusations joined the party, and I refuse to let Eric beat me at any more board games. So we're left with a fashion show to pass the time and maybe redeem this weekend and my reputation, not to mention my chances of securing a marriage proposal from my non-murderous lover."

Maddie doubted anyone would look forward to a fashion show, particularly one that highlighted their own limited weekend wardrobes, but she understood Dottie's perspective. Her reputation meant almost as much to her as her net worth, and Jason's importance couldn't be underestimated either. Maddie wasn't sure that preserving that reputation was a justification for letting someone get away with murder, but what about Dottie's other concern?

"You love him, don't you?"

Dottie gaped at the suggestion but didn't deny it.

"He called you Dottie."

"Lots of people call me Dottie."

"Up until this moment, exactly two people have called you Dottie and lived. You didn't even flinch when Jason said it."

"It's that keen observation that makes you such a good detective."

"That has to mean something."

"Perhaps it means I'm not willing to jeopardize a potentially lucrative union over the minor inconvenience of a sobriquet."

"Tell that to your ex-husband," she muttered, earning a glare.

"Or perhaps it means I don't want a spat with Jason to imperil your chances with Rebecca."

Now it was Maddie's turn to gawk. "I don't know what you're talking about."

"You saw her this morning. Do tell, little one, has she already enjoyed a workout today?"

"I refuse to answer that on the grounds that it's crass."

"I'll have to draw my own conclusions then and assume that you object to the fashion show, not because it won't serve your investigation but because you fear the repercussions on your love life."

"One kiss hardly equals a love life."

"There was a kiss? Why am I only hearing about this now?"

"Because I didn't want to wake you up to share my practically nonexistent news." Maddie cringed at the excited gleam in her friend's eyes. "How have I not learned to keep my mouth shut?" she grumbled.

"Do you mean during the kiss or after?" Dottie's smirk was maddening.

"I'm not saying I think I have any real chance with Rebecca. Let's face it, I'm not really the kind of girl who inspires women like her to come and get it."

"If she's into smart and beautiful women with questionable grooming practices, then you're exactly her type."

"But"—Maddie ignored the backhanded compliment—"on the extremely slim chance that she's interested in me, I'd rather not douse myself in Rebecca repellant in the form of humiliation."

"If she's still interested after your entrance on Friday night, you have nothing to worry about."

"Thanks for that. I feel so much better."

"Listen, sweets, either she likes you and won't be turned off by your runway debut, or she's not interested, and it doesn't matter. Either way, the show must go on."

"And if we still don't know who the killer is when it's over?"

"Then Carlisle and I will devote all our energies to unraveling this mystery with you."

Maddie supposed that was the best she could ask for from her remarkably stubborn friend. And she still had a few hours before the curtain rose on Murder Island Fashion Weekend. If she happened to catch the killer before then, perhaps she could escape whatever fate awaited her in the world's largest garment bag.

"You have a deal," she said, already knowing she would regret this decision.

CHAPTER SIXTEEN

When Maddie returned to her room, she eyed the garment bag critically. She couldn't believe she'd agreed to this ridiculous idea—as if it wasn't bad enough putting the Mystery of Murder Island on hold until Dottie was ready to help her, now she'd signed up for certain humiliation in the form of haute couture.

"Maybe it won't be so bad," she said, and as if to prove herself wrong, tugged at the zipper of the garment bag.

Slowly and horribly, a sea of blue fabric cascaded from the confines of the apparently magical bag. It was like a waterfall of fabric that threatened to flood the room. As the dress pooled around her feet, Maddie succumbed to a wave of panic.

The dress from Friday, the one by the up-and-coming designer (of tents as well as women's clothing, apparently), the nightmare apparel that had driven her to the comparative safety of high heels, her very own prêt-à-porter purgatory, had come back to haunt her. She backed away, shuddering.

"I have to get out of this somehow."

But how could she? She'd already agreed that the fashion show could go on, and she'd never reneged on a promise to Dottie, no matter how preposterous the request. She couldn't just back out now—unless the justification for the show no longer existed. What if, by some miracle, Maddie managed to catch the killer before showtime? Then they would no longer need the fashion show to ensnare the murderer, and Maddie would get a reprieve from her fate as a fashion victim.

Not that she truly believed Dottie would so easily bid adieu to her brilliant plan. Even if it was no longer necessary for catching the killer, it would still allegedly provide entertainment for her guests (though Maddie questioned the entertainment value of watching the same people they'd been trapped with for days parading around in the same clothes they'd had at their disposal all weekend). But if the show did still go on, perhaps catching a killer would earn her a "Get out of complete mortification" card. Or, if she was lucky, this confrontation with a killer would go about as well as they usually did, and a concussion or some other grievous injury would prevent her ignominious runway debut. At any rate, seeking out a multiple murderer was a better use of her time than fixating on the big blue haystack looming in her closet.

"What do I do now?" She looked to the dogs for help, but their only response was to bark at the odious dress currently terrorizing the room.

"If only barking at my problems would make them go away," she sighed, and stared at the dress, bewildered by what Dottie saw in it. "Why does it have to be so big? And blue. And hideous."

Seeking distance from her designer destiny, she paced the length of the room, considering her options. Mammon and Archer gave her their undivided attention while Ares chewed diligently on a Manolo Blahnik. "When did you get this?" Maddie gasped and, fearing both certain bowel obstruction as well as Cate's lethal response, she carefully swapped the pump for a tennis ball she had no memory of bringing into the room.

"You'll thank me when you don't get turned into a coat," she told the thieving Yorkipoo before returning to her antihumiliation mission. "This all started on Friday night, after everyone went to bed." Mammon refuted Maddie's claim with one of those quizzical, tilted-head looks dogs excel at. "I'm talking about the actual murders, not what inspired them."

To that, Archer lifted his eyebrows in a clear question. "If fewer people had reason to want Helen dead, motive might be more helpful." He sighed and rested his chin on his paws. "I'm not saying motive isn't important, buddy. I just don't think it's how we'll figure this one out." Though she believed the question of motive did have some merit, just not in Helen's case. "Why kill Timothy and the others? I'm assuming Helen died first and all the subsequent murders were because the killer was tying up loose ends."

It wasn't difficult to believe that Helen had been the intended target (for any number of reasons) and that Timothy had witnessed something that put the killer at risk of exposure. But how much could he have seen? He obviously wasn't killed in the wine cellar—the lack of blood or available axes made that apparent. Not to mention the superfluous effort of moving the body from the wine cellar to the teahouse. Unless Jason really was the killer, she didn't see why anyone would even consider lugging a body up the stairs and out of the mansion. The exertion and the risk were too great.

"Timothy must have run away, right?" Three tails thumped in apparent agreement, offering a small (and likely unsubstantiated) boost to her confidence. "But why did he leave the mansion full of people?" Had he simply trotted upstairs, he might still be alive and Maddie would have enjoyed a remarkably different weekend.

As she pondered these unanswerable questions, she paced across her room, the dogs' excitement waxing each time she approached the door (which presumably led to more enjoyable pursuits) and waning as she turned toward the closet and its ominous reminder of the need for urgency.

"And what about Chef Barbara?" she asked them, certain they knew as much as she did. "What threat did she pose? And why wait until the next day to kill her? I'm sure the killer was tired from chasing and axing Timothy, but this seems sort of like an 'in for a penny, in for a pound' situation, you know?"

If the dogs did know, they hid it well. Archer rose, stretched, turned himself in a circle and then resettled on the bed in almost the exact place he'd started from. Meanwhile, his sister and her diminutive beau snuggled closer and took turns licking each other's faces. It seemed she'd have to carry on without their input.

Had the chef confronted the killer? That hardly seemed like a wise decision, especially considering what happened to Timothy, but the opportunistic nature of the chef's murder suggested that, perhaps, this was exactly what had happened.

Maybe Chef Barbara tried her hand at blackmail. Almost everyone on the island had money, so it wasn't implausible to think she might have attempted to secure her future—in more ways than one. If so, she would have addressed the killer in private, making her vulnerable to his or her considerable rage.

As for Leslie, Maddie thought she probably sealed her fate when she admitted she feared for her life because of what she knew. Even though she claimed that was nothing, a person who'd committed three murders in two days wasn't likely to take her word for it.

But who had the opportunity to commit all of these heinous acts? And how would she root them out? She'd already searched for clues, more than once, and come up more or less empty. Aside from abject supplication to the ghost of Miss Marple, she was out of ideas.

A knock at her door intruded upon her thoughts, and though she hadn't been on the verge of a major breakthrough, she felt disproportionately irritated at the interruption. Half expecting to find Carlisle delivering another blow to Maddie's self-worth in the form of atrocious accessories to make her evening hell complete, she yanked the door open to find Castor fidgeting with the cuffs of his lavender dress shirt.

"Have you seen Ares? It's lunchtime, and he tends to misbehave if I don't respect his schedule. He stole my father's dentures once." His contrite expression made him almost likeable.

"I find that easy to believe." She held up the toothmark-dappled shoe and stepped aside to reveal the culprit.

"You had to target aspiring Imelda Marcos? You couldn't have gone for the drapes?" he gently scolded Ares, who showed neither interest nor remorse. "I'll get him out of your way."

"He's not bothering me. I know he has to eat, but if he wants to come back after lunch, he's more than welcome to stay with us. He seems to like it here." She gestured to the bed where Ares spooned with Mammon.

"We'll see."

He called his dog to him, and as Ares meandered across the room, stopping to sniff the invisible enticements he detected every other foot, the uncomfortable silence stretched out between them. Maddie cleared her throat and avoided eye contact, wishing she had a fast forward button. She was contemplating acting as a Yorkipoo taxi when she realized that this was a prime opportunity to talk to Castor alone.

"Castor?" She cleared her throat again, her confidence faltering under his unwavering gaze. "I'm sorry."

He stepped back, his face a toxic blend of curiosity and animosity. "What on earth could the ineffective detective have to be sorry for?"

"I never offered my condolences. I can't imagine how difficult losing your sister must be for you. I'm sorry."

His mouth agape, he seemed momentarily stupefied. In her minimal experience with him, she'd yet to see him at a loss for words, and this apparent vulnerability softened him, made him appear somewhat more human, but he recovered quickly.

"Water under the bridge, dog girl." He smiled thinly and turned to leave.

"You seem to be handling it remarkably well," she said. "If one of my sisters was murdered, especially when I was so close by, I'd be a mess. I'd do anything to find out who did it. You don't seem all that concerned."

"Nor would I be concerned about finding the sanitation worker who hauled away last week's trash."

"That's kind of harsh, don't you think? She was your sister."

"It must have escaped your keen notice that Helen and I didn't get along. I'm not sure why you think a bit of shared genetic material would make me immune to her entire lack of charm, but it didn't, not when we were children and certainly not now."

"What could she possibly have done to you to make you so indifferent to her death?"

"I don't think you have time for the full list."

"How about the abridged version?" she pushed. As unpleasant as Helen was, Maddie still couldn't fathom being so callous about the loss of her sister.

"Let's just say that she had a habit of sharing my misdeeds with our parents, yet she never got caught doing anything wrong."

"So, she was smarter than you? That's it?"

"What's your point?" He loomed over her in the doorway, his sneer oozing malice.

"Aren't you even a little sorry that she's dead? She was your twin, and she was murdered. It seems like you don't even care, like you wouldn't even have tried to stop the killer if you'd been there," she pressed.

"How could I have been there? The wine cellar was off limits, remember?"

"Even to her brother?"

"Especially to her brother."

"But what about the others—Timothy and Chef Barbara and Leslie?"

"What about them?"

"I guess I'm wondering what kind of man you are—the kind who helps in a crisis or the kind who hides?"

"I'm the kind of man who wants to be alone with his dog." At that he scooped Ares up in his arms and strode down the hall toward the stairs.

"That I understand," Maddie said to his retreating back.

She closed the door and turned to the dogs, who'd made themselves somehow more comfortable on the bed. In spite of the overwhelming urge to hide under the covers with them until the helicopter arrived in the morning, she clapped her hands together and announced, "I know what we have to do."

CHAPTER SEVENTEEN

"Let's go," Maddie called to Mammon and Archer and headed out the door, not at all confident that she wasn't making a grave mistake.

After all, she was about to confront a killer. Not that she would necessarily know it at the time—she was merely setting out to ask some questions. As her chat with Castor reminded her, it was the one tactic she'd as yet neglected to try this investigation. True, she wasn't a skilled interrogator. Her triumphs in this arena were sparse at best, but stumbling through a series of awkward conversations was preferable to waiting around to die (or, worse, to wear a pool cover masquerading as a dress).

At her command, the dogs leapt from the bed and trotted after her. Their exuberant obedience in that moment both buoyed her spirits and elevated her anxiety. While she embraced their animated approach to this adventure, she feared their excitement was more geared for a romp in the park than for security detail, especially considering their lackluster history as guard dogs (their owner and handler had both been murdered on their watch, after all). Taking that disquieting fact into consideration, she wondered, not for the first time, if she was needlessly putting herself in danger. Wouldn't it be terrible if her untimely demise interfered with the dogs' frisky playfulness?

"This is probably one of the stupidest things I've ever done. And I've done plenty of stupid things in my life. Agreeing to this weekend, for example," she said to her unwitting protectors. "Really, how likely is it that I'll get a chance to talk to any of these people alone? And even if I do, I doubt they'll just go ahead and confess. Presumably, three out of four murders this weekend have happened to cover up the original crime, so why would the murderer suddenly decide to fess up instead of using a nearby vase as a cudgel?"

The dogs looked at her quizzically but continued to follow her lead, a response that did little to calm her nerves. If only she had more in the way of backup than the world's least effective watchdogs. Should she somehow manage to crack the case while chatting with the guilty party, she didn't trust her entire lack of a poker face not to give her away, leaving her face-to-face with a violent and resourceful murderer. It would be just her luck to be bludgeoned to death with tasteless statuary while Mammon and Archer romped through the halls, oblivious to her distress.

"Normally, I'd ask Dottie to go with me or at least send her a text before I headed out on a potential suicide mission. But she's otherwise occupied." Apparently sensing this would be a lengthy delay, the dogs sat. "And I'm sure Carlisle is up to her eyeballs in demands from Dottie, so I don't even have my second-best option." She shook her head in disbelief. "I really need to expand my social circle if my second-best option is Carlisle, efficiency master and ninja-robot librarian extraordinaire. That means you guys are in charge of keeping me out of trouble. Can you handle that?"

As if pledging their agreement, Mammon and Archer wagged their tails in unison. Maddie, however, didn't trust that their loyalty wouldn't turn the second they saw a stick or some other canine enticement. Since she'd rather not die because her only protection found her less engaging than a squeaky toy, her first stop was the kitchen. Not that she expected to find any of her suspects there (really, what were the odds that Cate would overcome her aversion to domestic labor long enough to whip up an omelet?), but that's where the dog treats were kept, and she didn't really want to leave it to chance that the dogs didn't like the killer better than her.

"Remember this later," she told each of the pups as she dispensed generous helpings of beef jerky snacks without requesting any obedience in exchange.

Her security team adequately bribed, she grabbed the bag of treats as insurance and headed to the dining room. The dogs padded softly behind her, a perfect vantage point from which to witness Maddie's tragically comic death by expensive but tacky décor. The door to the dining room stood open, and she breezed in with a confidence she didn't feel. Just inside the doorway, she stopped. The dogs, however, continued moving forward until they collided with her legs, the force of their impact causing her to stumble forward and unleashing a klutzy domino effect involving two chairs and the sideboard.

Thankfully, the room was empty, a stark contrast to Friday night when ten of them had sat around the table enjoying a meal and sharing lively (if at times hostile) conversation. At the time, Maddie had been so consumed with her own awkwardness and embarrassment that she'd failed to fully appreciate what would turn out to be the high point of the weekend. As she righted herself and the furniture, she felt momentary relief that there'd been no one around to witness her most recent humiliation.

"I don't suppose I've used up my allotted clumsiness for the day," she sighed, thoughts of certain fashion show disaster filling her head.

All evidence of her latest clash with gravity cleaned up, she led her too-eager attendants toward the lounge.

"Let's try to be a little more graceful," she admonished the dogs. "If we do find someone to interrogate, I just think the conversation will go better if I'm not facedown on the floor under a pile of accent pillows. Got it?"

The dogs spun in a circle, their tails whipping furiously behind them, imperiling any unsecured objects in their path. Whether they understood or were simply excited by the smell of the treats, Maddie didn't know. Still, feeling optimistic about her chances of staying upright, she entered the lounge and again stopped short (this time narrowly avoiding a canine pileup) when she found Cate sprawled on a tufted, paisley-patterned chesterfield, flipping through the pages of a fashion magazine. She'd kicked off her pumps, which lay untidily on the floral print rug, and her cream-colored pantsuit acted like an oasis for the senses, a tiny patch of relief from the visual assault of Helen's objectionable aesthetic.

Cate glanced up from her magazine, a perplexed scowl marring her face. "Were you just talking to the dogs?"

"They're surprisingly good listeners."

"How are they at hasty exits?" Her attention had already returned to the glossy pages of her magazine.

Ignoring Cate's habitual rudeness, Maddie fixed an excessively cheery expression on her face and invited herself to join Cate on the couch. "How did you sleep?" she chirped, startling herself and her target.

"Is this some sort of guest satisfaction survey?" Cate spoke to the pages in front of her, her disinterest clear.

"Just friendly conversation." Maddie tried again unsuccessfully to compete with the allure of the magazine. "Or maybe not so friendly," she muttered to Archer, who yawned and rested his large head on her thigh. Mammon turned herself in a circle and plopped onto the rug at Maddie's feet. "I had trouble sleeping, myself."

"How nice." Cate flipped the page and pivoted away from her unwanted company.

"I was so restless that I actually had to take a walk in the middle of the night." She scrutinized Cate's profile, but aside from a stifled yawn, saw no indication that the woman was even listening.

"Naturally I was shocked to find there was another murder while I was out of my room. If I had been just a minute or two earlier, I might have seen who did it."

At that, Cate turned to face Maddie, mouth agape. Her magazine fell to her lap. "Another murder? My god, how did I end up on this miserable island?"

Maddie watched as Cate's emotions played across her face—her shock seemed self-absorbed but genuine. If only narcissism was a viable alibi. She resisted the urge to answer "Karma," and instead pushed forward with her ill-conceived inquiry. "I guess that's what's got me wondering about how you slept last night. Maybe you had no trouble at all, or maybe you paid a visit to the third floor."

"The third floor? What on earth would I find interesting about the third floor?"

"Leslie." Cate stared at her blankly, as if she honestly couldn't remember who that was. "The maid. And most recent murder victim."

"I can't believe we wasted so much time looking for her."

Maddie tamped down her distaste and instead opted to press her luck. "Again, I'm wondering how you slept last night, Cate?"

At that, anger flashed in Cate's eyes, and Maddie inched farther away, bracing for impact. At the very least, she expected a hearty slap, but she couldn't help but notice the various potential weapons within reach of the irate woman sitting across from her. She nudged Archer, hoping to encourage if not an act of bravery, at least an intimidating growl. Instead, she inspired a look of such sheer annoyance she worried he'd swear allegiance to Cate just to get even. Cate's fingers tightened around her magazine, but before she could do more than sputter in her rage, Jason appeared from nowhere and stood towering over them like a well-groomed redwood. He flipped his hair, still damp from the shower, out of his eyes and smiled broadly at the women as the scent of Coach for Men wafted through the room, surrounding them like a penumbra of fragrance.

"We were having a private conversation." Maddie attempted to discourage him from overstaying his welcome.

"About what?"

"Something *private*," she stressed the word, hoping he would take the rather large hint.

Instead, he squeezed himself between the women, making himself far too comfortable for her liking. "Don't let me stop you."

"Too late," she muttered.

"We weren't talking about anything important," Cate said. She faced him and laid her hand on his forearm.

To his credit, Jason shifted out of her reach. Unfortunately, his bulk tested the limitations of the couch, and Maddie found herself pinned between his expansive back and the arm of the chesterfield. Her security team, meanwhile, abandoned her and rested at Jason's feet, gazing up at him adoringly. So much for treat-based loyalty.

"It seemed important to me." Maddie popped her head out from behind Jason's back.

"You also think the natural look is your friend. You know, my company, Julieta, makes an incredible under-eye serum and concealer. We could wipe out those bags under your eyes."

Maddie groaned inwardly, wondering what sins of her past had subjected her to the Dottie of cosmetics. "You do remember that I was hit in the face, right?"

"I can't imagine it was the first time," Cate sneered.

"What does any of this have to do with the murders?" Maddie ground her teeth in frustration.

"You were talking about the murders?" Jason asked excitedly, his aspirations of investigative glory on full display.

"What else has anyone talked about this weekend? Frankly, it's grown tiresome." She rose and gathered her belongings. "If you'll excuse me, I'm going to go do something interesting."

"Good luck," Jason called after her as she exited the room.

"Now I'm never going to get any answers from her." Maddie turned on him as soon as Cate was gone.

"Did you really think you were likely to?"

"No," she admitted and drooped against the back of the couch. "What are you doing here anyway?"

"Dottie asked me to keep an eye on you."

"Terrific. But I don't need a bodyguard." She rose and took a step toward the door. Jason followed.

"She told me you'd say that and that I should ignore you." He shrugged and looked almost apologetic. "She's worried about you. Is that so wrong?"

"I appreciate the concern, but the dogs and I will be just fine on our own." She glanced toward her top-notch security detail, half of which was invested in licking his nether regions while his sister paced the length of a nearby loveseat, rubbing her sides along the cushions and grunting in obvious pleasure.

"Why are you so dead set against having my help?"

"Why would I take a suspect with me to grill other suspects?"

"You think I killed three people?"

"I think you could have," she spoke without conviction. Even if she hadn't already begun to doubt his guilt, the fact that he'd said three people instead of four gave her pause. True, he could simply be a skillful liar—he was a professional performer, after all—but he seemed too doltishly genuine to be that duplicitous.

"I had nothing to do with any of those deaths."

"Then how did you get that cut on your arm?"

"I broke a wineglass on Friday night."

"Were you in the wine cellar at the time?"

"Actually, I was with your best friend at the time. I'd rather not share any more details than that."

In spite of herself, Maddie appreciated his gentlemanly consideration, if for no other reason than she wouldn't be exposed to any more details of Dottie's robust sex life than necessary.

"Is that where you were when Helen and Timothy were killed?"

"Yes." She wanted to interpret his complete lack of hesitation as a sign of his innocence. Had he been guilty, he probably would have taken a minute to compose a lie. Unless, of course, he'd anticipated this moment. On top of that, she'd basically fed him an alibi, and he took it, an alibi that couldn't be verified thanks to Dottie's eternal mission to be well rested.

"What about when Chef Barbara was killed? Where were you then?"

"Probably moving Timothy's body to the wine cellar or cleaning up after that. I'm not sure exactly when she died."

"Neither am I," she admitted. "But you were lurking in the hall around the time Leslie died."

"I wasn't lurking—wait, what happened to Leslie?" He sank back onto the chesterfield, the news of Leslie's demise seemingly having blindsided him.

"She was murdered last night," she said and shared the details, all the while watching his face for any signs of guilt. All she saw was a man in pain. Sadness and disbelief clouded his features before he dropped his head into his hands.

"And you *were* just outside her door when I found her, so you can see why I might find you suspicious."

"I had no idea." He shook his head ruefully then rose, a look of fierce determination in his eyes. "We have to catch whoever did this."

"What do you think I've been trying to do for the past twenty-four hours?"

"So, what's our next move?" He bounced a little on his toes, his eagerness to right wrongs both endearing and irritating.

"I'm going to talk to the other suspects. You're going to go back to whatever you were doing before you interrupted me." Again, she moved toward the door.

"No way am I letting you go alone." Jason effortlessly kept pace with her, not a difficult feat for a man who was a full foot taller.

"I don't need your protection," she growled.

"Maybe not, but you do need my help."

"I'm interrogating suspects not opening pickle jars."

"Suspects who already don't trust you. How far do you think you're going to get with a bunch of people who believe you're out to get them?"

"But you expect them to talk to you?" she snapped, irked by the validity of his point.

"You saw how Cate responded to me." He shrugged again, as if his charm were an indisputable fact. "People like me."

"I'm not sure Florence will succumb to your charms so easily. Souped-up manly virility isn't really her cup of tea."

"That hasn't stopped you from talking to me, has it? And you were already hostile when we started this conversation."

She opened her mouth to argue but had no rebuttal. "Fine. Let's go. But try not to get in the way."

She marched ahead, hoping to lose him during the brief walk from the lounge to the neighboring library, but since his legs were roughly the same length as her entire body, he easily kept pace with her. The dogs, still not aware of the plan, raced past the library door and slid to a graceless stop two doors down. As they scrambled to rejoin the pack, the clamor of their nails on the hardwood floor effectively announced their impending arrival to anyone who might be in the room.

Inside the room, Florence sat in a leather chair, documents spread out across nearby furniture and the floor around her. An open laptop rested on her thighs, her hands hovering over the keyboard, and she glanced at them over the tops of her tortoiseshell reading glasses, her expression resting somewhere between annoyance and curiosity. The dogs, interpreting that as an invitation, bounded to her, heedless of the very important paperwork they trampled en route to the unwilling recipient of their slobbery kisses.

"Can you do something about this?" she cried, an action she likely regretted once Archer's tongue slipped inside her open mouth.

Maddie struggled to pull the dogs away, and when she turned to Jason for help wrangling the beasts, she saw that he was fighting to contain his laughter. His shoulders shook, his face was red, and his lips were pressed tightly together. In spite of her irritation, she found him immensely likeable in that moment.

"Can I help you with something, or did you interrupt me for the fun of it?" Florence wiped at her drool-dampened face aggressively.

"We didn't mean to intrude. The dogs just got away from us," Maddie said, impressed with her facile lie. "I'm just curious, why are you working?" Florence merely glowered before turning her attention back to the laptop in front of her. "I would think you'd be relieved now that Helen's gone," Maddie pressed. "No one is pressuring you to work on your vacation. You could just relax and enjoy the rest of the weekend."

"What part of this weekend has been enjoyable to you? The constant threat of death or the incessant bickering?"

"I like the scenery myself," Jason chimed in.

"I'll be sure to enjoy it once I've finished here. Now if you'll excuse me—"

"Finished what?" Maddie asked.

"Excuse me?"

"I'm just wondering what you could possibly be working on with no access to the Internet or the outside world."

"Not that it's any of your business, but I'm trying to draft a press release. The head of Andreas Corp. has died rather unexpectedly. The company should make a statement." She again looked to the glowing screen before her.

"Surely that could wait. No one knows except for the people on this island."

"I need to have this ready to go the second I get back to civilization, so no, it can't wait."

"But wouldn't it be better to make a more complete statement? Maybe say something about who did it?"

"Have you figured that out?" Florence leaned forward a little, as if eager to learn of any developments in Maddie's investigation. Whether that eagerness was due to guilt or curiosity, Maddie couldn't say.

"Not yet. I'm still trying to find out where everyone was during the murders."

"Are you asking for my alibi?"

"Alibis, plural, actually."

A silent, tense moment passed as Florence narrowed her eyes and frowned. Maddie tightened her grip on the dogs' collars, grateful for their nearness (even if the only protection they offered was in the form of slobber).

"On Friday night, I was alone in my room trying to get cell reception, and when the chef was killed, I'd guess I was changing into dry clothes or soaking my feet. Now, if there's nothing else—"

"Just one more thing." Jason leaned close to Florence and spoke in his best grizzled TV detective voice. "Where were you last night when Leslie was killed?"

She gasped, her shock evident. "That poor girl," she said, her voice barely a whisper. Without warning, her shock turned to anger. "Why am I only hearing about this now? We should have been told immediately."

"We're the ones asking the questions here." Jason had clearly embraced his self-appointed role of gumshoe.

Unintimidated by his performance, Florence rose, and standing as tall as possible for a five-foot-nothing woman, stared him down. "I didn't kill anyone, but if you don't get out of here and let me get back to work, that might change."

"That's what you call being helpful?" Maddie snarled once the door closed behind them. "Now she's even more defensive."

"It's not as if you were getting anywhere with your questions. And now we know she has a lousy alibi."

"That we have no way of disproving or verifying," she said, her frustration and disappointment growing. "Just try not to be so charming when we find Eric."

Even having met him only two days earlier, Maddie already knew the most likely place to find Eric, and so, with her hodgepodge security detail in tow, she marched out the back door, eager to put an end to Jason's contributions to her case (even though the alternative landed her squarely in Dottie's fashion crosshairs). As they trudged across the drenched and branch-strewn lawn, their feet squelching with every step, she half-hoped they'd encounter a sturdy bough at roughly the same height as Jason's forehead, but knowing her luck, the branch would simply snap upon impact with his skull, and Archer would run off with his fabulous new toy, leaving her in the sizeable hands of her would-be protector and his illusions of PI glory.

"How serious are you about Dottie?" she asked as they made their cautious way through a particularly dense patch of debris from the surrounding foliage.

"Are we having the intentions talk?" He extended a meaty hand to help her over a thick tree limb, and she reluctantly accepted it.

"Is that a problem?" she challenged. He might meet the "not a murderer" criterion for dating her best friend, but if he was going to be a more constant presence in Dottie's life, then Maddie needed to know more about him.

"Not at all. I appreciate your concern for your friend."

He fell silent and she grew impatient waiting for an answer. "And?"

"And I enjoy spending time with her. I hope to do more of that."

"In a marital capacity?" If he was surprised by her directness, he didn't show it. In fact, that damn smile reappeared at twice its charming strength.

"You don't mess around, do you?"

"Not when it comes to the people I love."

"Well, I'm not messing around either."

His somewhat ambiguous answer left her with about a dozen follow-up questions, none of which she had time to ask as they approached their destination.

Maddie was in no way surprised to find Eric in the stables. She was, however, taken somewhat aback by his activities. He was sweeping up debris (in crisply pressed black dress slacks, no less). Every now and then, he would kneel in the muck underfoot to scrutinize the floor or tap on the wall as if checking the soundness of the structure. To anyone who hadn't grown up with a contractor for a father, he probably looked fairly knowledgeable.

However, as if determined to undermine all illusions of his competence, he fumbled with a tape measure, extending the blade several times before letting it slip from his fingers and snap back into its case. Unfortunately, by the time he'd mastered the fine art of the thumb lock, he'd managed to expose a good ten feet of the ruler and now wielded it like an ineffective rapier. He wasn't even anywhere near a wall, window or other structure that could conceivably be measured.

"What are you doing, man?"

Eric shrieked and dropped his tool, releasing the lock and once again sending the blade coiling back inside its case at a blistering pace. The metallic zipping of the blade's retreat ended in a final snap that resulted in a tiny, alarmed leap from Eric. Without even a trace of the embarrassment he surely should have felt in that moment, he turned to face them.

"I'm assessing the damage from the storm. I want to ensure that the stables are safe and ready for the horses."

"Are you expecting a visit from equestrian Santa Claus?" Maddie's glance swept the entirety of the decidedly horse-less stables, wondering what she was missing.

Eric's sharp crack of laughter startled her, and she took a step closer to Jason. Meanwhile, the remainder of her bodyguards loped past, each holding one end of a fallen branch in their mouths.

"I've been thinking this place would be a great asset for the rescue, so I was going to put in an offer, but after the storm last night, I need to make sure the horses will be safe." He resumed his thorough-in-appearance-only examination of the structure, and Maddie resisted the urge to help him

"You want to buy the island?"

"Well, Helen doesn't need it anymore, and Castor needs the money more than the property. Unpleasant murder associations aside, it's a lovely spot, and given its recent history, I could probably get a great deal on it."

"No doubt," she said, her thoughts torn between Eric's macabre opportunism and the chance that rather than taking advantage of Helen's demise, he'd actually brought it about for exactly this reason. "When did you first realize this would be an asset?"

"Gosh, I thought so from the moment I first saw the place." He placed the end of the tape measure in the dead center of the stable partition closest to him and extended it as far as his arm would reach, as if such a measurement would be in any way useful.

"So, on Friday?"

"Oh no. This isn't my first visit." He repeated his pointless measuring just a few steps to the left. "I've visited the island several times before now."

"And did you talk to Helen about buying it?"

"Repeatedly. I think that's why she kept inviting me here. She liked to broadcast her wealth, and the more she knew one of her possessions appealed to someone, the more she flaunted it."

"How badly did you want this island?" Jason asked. He leaned in close to Eric, using his height advantage to intimidating effect. Eric, however, remained oblivious.

"My offer was well above the fair market value of the property. But you know Helen. She always wanted more." Eric bent to pick up an errant water bucket but stopped midstoop and looked to Jason. "How do you work out?"

Jason stared at him blankly, probably trying to make some sense out of the non-sequitur question.

"I have a friend who wants to get in better shape," Eric clarified, "but he doesn't know what to do when he goes to the gym. He thought maybe you would have some advice."

"You should join me for my workout tomorrow. I'll show you what to do, you know, for your friend."

As Jason flexed inadvertently and Eric beamed over being included by the cool kid, Maddie's mind raced. Eric had ample motive for wanting Helen dead, and though he seemed morally capable of murder, she doubted he was physically able to kill anyone, at least not in a way that utilized tools of any kind. She honestly wasn't sure he would have known which side of the pillow to smother Leslie with, so how likely was it that his proficiency with an ax was enough to end Timothy's life? Still, she wasn't willing to write him off as a suspect just for perceived incompetence. After all, he could be faking it.

"I hate to interrupt this very important conversation, but can we get back to what we were talking about before bodybuilding banter began?"

Eric looked genuinely confused. "I thought we were done with that."

"Not even close," Maddie said.

"Okay then. What else did you want to know about Helen not selling this property?"

"Well, we were done with *that*," Maddie admitted. "But I had other questions that had nothing to do with calisthenics or plyometrics."

"Plyo-what?" Eric's perplexed expression deepened, and he looked to Jason for help.

"It's really not that complicated." Jason moved to demonstrate, but Maddie cleared her throat pointedly. "I'll show you tomorrow."

"Will Rebecca be there too?" Eric asked, and Maddie struggled not to scream in frustration.

"Can we please focus?" she asked through gritted teeth.

"There you are. Why aren't you dressed yet?"

All three of them spun to see Carlisle standing in the doorway, clipboard in hand. Her usually stern expression was dialed to eleven.

"The show starts in an hour, and you aren't even close to ready for inspection," she tutted in Maddie's general direction.

"Inspection? I can dress myself."

"In the broadest sense, yes, but that won't do today. Let's go." She gestured toward the main house, and both men exited. With nightmare visions of an embarrassment of blue fabric swirling through her mind, Maddie reluctantly followed.

CHAPTER EIGHTEEN

Maddie carefully avoided her reflection in the mirror. Not that she couldn't see her billowing contribution to Dottie's entertainment without it. With every move she made, the endless yards of fabric rustled and flowed around her, the profuse circumference of each of her sleeves a constant reminder of her current fashion-based predicament. She didn't see how any amount of zhuzhing, even at Dottie's expert hands, could improve her appearance (unless said attentions culminated in changing to jeans and a T-shirt and setting the dress on fire). Physically and emotionally uncomfortable, she sat on her bed and waited for the not-at-all humiliating inspection.

And as if not being trusted to don a dress correctly wasn't bad enough, she'd somehow managed to go backward in her investigation. Instead of eliminating suspects and finding answers, she'd uncovered yet another motive for Helen's murder and done a spectacular job of alienating almost everyone in the process—except for Eric, who was too consumed with his potential real estate acquisition and playing Contractor Make Believe to realize he was a suspect.

She didn't dare ask how things could get any worse. Why tempt fate?

A glance at her watch told her she still had twenty minutes or so before her unveiling as blue Grimace, more if Dottie stayed true to her habitually belated self. Maybe, if Maddie's fortune took a drastic turn for the better, she could figure this out before anyone saw her. True, she didn't know much more than when she set off on her adventure (except that Mammon and Archer should not be entrusted with anyone's safety), but maybe she didn't need new information. Maybe she simply needed to reconsider what she already knew.

"There must be something I'm missing," she grumbled and fell back on the bed, the great *whoosh* of fabric drowning out her voice. "I'm dealing with businesspeople and socialites, not seasoned criminals. There's no way that whoever did this didn't make some mistake or leave behind some trace of who they are. If only I could figure out what that was."

Before she could further contemplate the case, the door flew open, and Dottie stood in the doorway, looking effortlessly elegant in a sleek black dress that accentuated her many assets. It seemed a little over the top to Maddie, but what would Dottie be if not over the top?

"Why am I not surprised to find you lounging about rather than getting ready?"

"I'm not lounging, I'm despondent. And I thought I was ready."

"Sweet potato, simply being clothed is hardly sufficient for an event of this magnitude."

Dottie stood at the side of the bed, staring down at her. She had that calculating look in her eye, the one that generally preceded a makeover campaign that Maddie had no interest in or patience to deal with in that moment. She was like a human dark cloud, and just the thought of Dottie-mandated primping filled Maddie with dread.

"What on earth do you have to be despondent over?"

"You mean aside from all the deaths and my total inability to catch a break in this case?"

"That?" She fluttered her fingers in the air as if the harsh reality of their situation could be shooed away like an annoying insect. "We'll get to the bottom of it after we've taken a moment to appreciate fine apparel. To that end, I'm relieved to see that Jason kept you free from harm, in spite of your determination to endanger yourself."

"The only thing I was in danger of was finding answers to my questions." Maddie didn't bother moving from her defeated position on the bed.

"I know you, Moon Pie. I needed to make sure you didn't get yourself killed just to avoid haute couture."

"I'd settle for maimed if it got me out of this." She gestured to her outfit and instantly felt the fan effect of moving her sail-like sleeves.

"Try not to rumple your gown, pumpkin bread. We don't want you looking like a vagrant."

"I'm not sure *vagrant* is exactly the takeaway anyone would get. Walking blue haystack or possibly giant sea spray might be more accurate."

"Don't be petulant, Matilda. It's unseemly."

"And *that* would be embarrassing."

"You're exceptionally snarky today."

"Must be all the stress-relieving qualities of this relaxing weekend getaway."

"Honestly, Maddie, would it kill you to show just a little gratitude for the honor I'm bestowing on you? I know you don't appreciate fashion—you make that abundantly clear on a daily, denim-clad basis. Nevertheless, I've made you the spotlight of this little fashion show. The least you could do is cooperate." She grabbed Maddie's wrist and hoisted her to her feet. Dottie's judgmental frown coincided with her scrutiny of Maddie's obviously disappointing appearance. "Did you neglect your grooming just to spite me? Hairbrushes aren't just for show, urchin. You can embrace the bohemian look on your own time."

"I'm the spotlight now? I thought this was just a ruse to see whose pin is missing."

"But we know that's a red herring." She turned Maddie's head from side to side, an ominously critical look in her eye.

"How so?" She tried to squirm out of Dottie's grasp, but her friend held tight.

"Jason's pin is missing, and he can't possibly be the guilty party. Ergo, the pin is meaningless."

"Meaningless might be an exaggeration."

"Either way, the focus of the fashion show has shifted. Now, it's an exhibition of daring apparel, and you, my dear, are the centerpiece. All eyes will be on you."

"Terrific," Maddie grumbled, pondering her chances of contracting botulism in the next fifteen minutes.

"Fear not, honeysuckle, the dress will be the true star. All you have to do is walk without falling for two minutes. You can handle that, can't you, champ?"

Even as she issued her reassurances that Maddie's role was mostly that of moving mannequin, Dottie opened her cosmetics case, ready to do battle with Maddie's apparently lackluster complexion.

"What are you doing?" she asked, somewhat unnecessarily.

"What you've clearly neglected to do." She brandished her concealer brush like a weapon, but Maddie dodged her thrust.

"Why do I have to wear makeup?"

"Why do you resist beautification at every turn?"

"It's just not me." A fact she felt her best friend should know.

"And that's the point. Tonight, you get to be someone you're not. It's like Halloween for a more discerning class of people. Embrace the transformation, toots."

"Maybe you should have chosen a different model, someone who doesn't need to be transformed."

"I never said you *need* to be transformed, but perhaps there's someone here on the island who would appreciate seeing a different side of you. Maybe someone you might be interested in canoodling with." Fighting her inevitable blush, Maddie quickly looked away. "Unless you already have. Have you canoodled? Am I out of the canoodling loop?"

"There's been no canoodling," she answered, still not meeting her friend's gaze. Even though she and Rebecca had done nothing more than kiss (which in Dottie's world came nowhere near the realm of canoodling), she still felt like she was getting off on a technicality.

"That's sure to change the moment you appear on the runway. Once Rebecca lays eyes on you, she'll have no choice but to act."

"That's what I'm afraid of."

"Trust me, sugar bear. You have nothing to worry about. You and this dress were made for each other." Considering the monstrosity currently circumfusing her body, Maddie tried not to be offended. "It's the epitome of fun and daring, two words that apply to you when you let yourself cut loose a little. Plus, it showcases those stunning legs of yours."

Maddie attempted to look at her legs, but the profusion of fabric between her and the floor prevented her from seeing them as Dottie might.

"Trust me, they're gorgeous. And if you'll just allow me to smooth out these rough edges of yours"—she again turned to her cosmetics case—"you'll be beyond irresistible."

"But if all eyes are going to be on this gown, do we even need to worry about my face?"

"Blasphemy," Dottie gasped and dropped her makeup brush.

"I'm just saying that what little time we have left to prepare should be focused on the true star of the evening." She gestured to the miles of sky-blue cloth she had accepted as her fate.

"Can we at least cover this bruising?"

"Do you really trust yourself to stop there?"

"You may have a point."

As Dottie relented and abandoned her cosmetics case, Maddie basked in her relief. For most, successful cosmetics evasive maneuvers would hardly be worth celebrating, but she seldom swayed Dottie's course, especially when it came to matters of beauty. And considering the weekend of failures she was currently mired in, Maddie intended to savor this small victory. She knew better than to gloat, however, and instead she turned Dottie's attention back to the evening's lamentable festivities.

"As the spotlight, does that mean I go first?" She held on to the slender hope that she could minimize the number of eyes on her and her magnificent swell of cloth.

"And deny others the pleasure of designer excellence?" She tsked. "Lambchop, you are the pièce de résistance, the moment everyone will be waiting for. You are the grand finale. That means that sitting, slouching, leaning, eating or drinking are verboten before your emergence upon the fashion scene."

"Am I allowed to breathe?"

"If you can do so without jostling the fabric." Dottie poked and prodded the layers of linen, stepping back and contemplating her efforts every so often. After one final adjustment, she clapped her finely manicured hands together and declared the look a success. "I've done exceptional work here. If only I had a celebratory cocktail."

As if summoned by Dottie's magic words, Carlisle appeared in the room, clipboard in one hand, dirty martini in the other. Maddie noted with something close to envy that Carlisle remained comfortably dressed in her usual sweater set. Evidently the upside of being at Dottie's beck and call was the unexpected bonus of remaining in the shadows.

"You're a godsend, Carlisle." After a hearty swallow, she produced a brush seemingly from nowhere and began doing battle with Maddie's thick, unruly curls.

"I thought you were finished."

"With the dress, apple tart. You may have swayed me where cosmetics are concerned, but on the matter of your hair, I am resolute. Your standard ponytail would besmirch the integrity of this event. Now stand still and enjoy your metamorphosis."

"I'd enjoy it more with a topical analgesic," she said through gritted teeth.

"Beauty is pain," Dottie admonished her, and continued her assault on Maddie's scalp. "Carlisle, please tell me we're on schedule. I can't abide tardiness."

Maddie savored her subsequent eye roll.

"Almost everything is in order, Ms. Hunter. There is one minor hiccup, however."

"Do we have to postpone the show?" Maddie asked hopefully.

"Hush, muffin. Details please, Carlisle."

"Cate can't find her Ferragamo foulard. Apparently, it ties the whole outfit together, and she refuses to go on until it's been returned."

"Returned? She thinks it's been stolen?" Maddie asked. She had no idea what a Ferragamo foulard was. Nevertheless, she felt confident no human on the island would be inclined to steal one.

"She has suggested that as a possibility."

The less-than-gentle tugging on Maddie's scalp stopped abruptly, and she clung to a slender thread of hope that Dottie would abandon her current role of hairdresser and that her hair was in no way an ostentatious match to the spectacle of her attire.

"First murders, now petty theft. If this gets out, it will ruin my stellar reputation."

"She probably just hasn't looked through the right pile of clothes yet," Maddie said, reflecting on the disarray of Cate's room.

Considering that everything was out of place, it was remarkable that Cate had even located her dress. Maddie shuddered at the thought of returning to that mess to help locate the missing item (one trip into that disheveled hell was enough to give her hives), but if it delayed her runway debut, even for a few minutes, she was open to the possibility. And at least this time there would be proper lighting, not like last night's search for Leslie.

"Last night's search," she muttered as pieces began falling into place.

"What about last night's search, lemon twist?"

"I know who the killer is," she gasped, realization dawning. "And I think I know how to prove it."

"If this is some kind of trick to get out of the fashion show—"

"I promise it's not, but I do need to check on a couple of things, so just stall and distract everyone until I get back."

As she dashed out of the room, hopeful that they would finally be putting this nightmare behind them, she heard Dottie call after her, "Slow down, pet. That frock is not intended for athletic purposes."

CHAPTER NINETEEN

Fifteen minutes later, having found what she needed, Maddie snuck through the back door of the ballroom and discovered the fashion show already in progress (much to her relief). That wasn't what she'd intended when she told Dottie to stall, but she couldn't say she was sorry to have missed out on the "fun" of watching Cate parade across an improvised runway in a shimmering, diaphanous gown. Having finished her moment in the spotlight, she joined Florence (wearing yet another staid brown dress) in the small audience. The latter woman shifted her weight from one leg to the other, her sensible flats being no match for the swollen feet she'd stuffed into them. Meanwhile, Eric fidgeted with his horseshoe cufflinks and gazed longingly at Rebecca, a fixation for which Maddie could hardly blame him.

Whether in the spirit of the event or at Dottie's specific request, Rebecca had ditched her usual slacks in favor of a sleeveless burgundy dress with a plunging neckline that momentarily drew Maddie's attention away from the task at hand. Forcing herself to tear her eyes away, she spotted Dottie to the right of the stage with an admittedly dapper-looking

Jason. She leaned into him slightly, welcoming the protective arm around her waist, and in spite of the otherwise nightmarish situation in which they found themselves, Maddie couldn't help but take a moment to appreciate her friend's happiness.

She was pleased to see Carlisle and her ever-present clipboard tucked away from the crowd, sitting at a small table in the back of the room. The table held neat stacks of paper, a camera and Carlisle's trusty clipboard, and she seemed to be dividing her attention equally among the papers, the clipboard and the fashion show. Maddie imagined that, if they hadn't been pressed for time and resources, Carlisle would be at the helm of a sound board while simultaneously operating a spotlight. As it was, she settled for consulting her copious notes and snapping photos. Despite the risks of interrupting Carlisle when she was multitasking, Maddie approached, crossing her fingers that Carlisle's pathological efficiency would work in her favor for once.

A smattering of applause coincided with her arrival at Carlisle's side, and Maddie turned to see Castor in his aubergine jacket, prancing onstage for the small crowd. At that distance (and with her degree of disinterest in haberdashery), she couldn't tell if he wore the same suit coat he'd worn on Friday or if the man simply had a surplus of purple attire. Either way, she spotted no pin on his lapel, thus proving both her point that the fashion show was a silly idea and Dottie's claim that the pin itself was moot. Fortunately, she'd found another way to unmask the killer.

"You're late." Carlisle's testy voice startled Maddie, and she turned to find the dour-faced assistant frowning at her. "Ms. Hunter has been distraught by the possibility that you would shirk your responsibilities."

"I can tell," Maddie said as Dottie threw her head back and laughed.

"Did you at least find what you were looking for?"

"That kind of depends on you."

Her sour expression shifted to something closer to pleased. "What about me?"

"When you inventoried the property on Friday, did you include the wine cellar?"

"Naturally." Carlisle sounded offended that Maddie would suspect her of unsatisfactory work.

"Please tell me you didn't skip the décor."

"I included everything."

Offering a silent prayer of thanks to the gods of amateur sleuthing, she hoped she wasn't about to press her luck with her next question. "Do you have the inventory with you, by chance?"

"You want to see that now?" Too anxious to speak, Maddie nodded vigorously. "Why are you suddenly taking an interest in the mundane aspects of my job?"

"Because I'm thinking of changing careers," she deadpanned. "Now please tell me you have it with you."

She glowered at Maddie over the rims of her glasses for a moment before turning her attention to the papers on the clipboard that Maddie swore she'd never mock again. Half an eternity passed as Carlisle's fingers moved nimbly through the pages. When she finally located the relevant section, the euphoria Maddie felt far exceeded the response warranted by a detailed rundown of a dead woman's possessions.

"I also have photographs if you need them." Carlisle flipped to the wine cellar portion of the inventory and directed Maddie's attention to the pertinent portion of her work.

"You really are a godsend." Maddie could have kissed her. "Carlisle, you've saved the day."

"That's hardly a surprise," Carlisle said matter-of-factly.

Too preoccupied with finally ending this case to comment on Carlisle's peculiar appropriation of her boss's near total lack of humility, Maddie left the self-satisfied assistant to her note taking and moved toward the other end of the room. She carried with her Carlisle's inventory, the wholly circumstantial evidence she'd picked up on her earlier stop, and the absolute certainty that she was right. That didn't amount to much in the eyes of the law, but if she played her cards right, she could exchange this bit of non-proof for a confession.

Her heart pounded and her hands trembled as she neared the group around the small stage where Castor entertained the audience with his antics. Looking at the cluster of people whose feelings for her ranged from affection to indifference to seething hostility, she felt oddly comforted knowing that at least she wouldn't be confronting the killer alone. Not that she trusted most of them to protect her should the accused turn violent, but perhaps the mere presence of seven other witnesses would curb any murderous impulses. Who knew? She might even wrap up this case without serious injury.

She felt a cold nose nudging her right arm and glanced down to see Archer, dressed for the occasion in a blue plaid bowtie, looking up at her reassuringly. To her left stood Mammon and Ares, sporting a floral collar and lavender gingham bowtie respectively. She paused to pet each of them, beyond thankful for their unexpected show of support, earning herself an affectionate if sloppy dog facial in the process.

Her courage properly bolstered, she insinuated herself into the group and watched as Castor removed his jacket and tossed it over his shoulder in something of a devil-may-care attitude. Obviously savoring the attention, he vamped it up for the audience, strutting and spinning. When he saw Maddie, he stopped midtwirl, his jaw dropped and for once, he seemed to be at a loss for words. Maybe Dottie hadn't been entirely wrong about the magical properties of her dress.

"Lemon drop, you've completely blown your entrance."

Rebecca's mouth dropped open, her astonishment plain. "You look—"

"Don't say stupid. I already know."

"I was going to say healthy."

"Surprisingly healthy." Cate offered a rare bit of positive (if confusing) feedback.

"Do I want to know what they're talking about?" Maddie asked Dottie.

"I may have explained away your absence by saying that you were experiencing a touch of gastrointestinal distress."

"You couldn't have gone with 'The zipper is stuck'?"

"And tarnish a young designer's reputation?"

"How considerate," Maddie said through clenched teeth, regretting the carte blanche she'd given her overly dramatic friend. "I thought you were going to stall."

"Fashion waits for no one, angel. I take it your mission was a success."

"It was."

"What mission? And why would she need to stall?" Rebecca asked. She turned to Maddie and whispered, "What's going on?"

"My question exactly. Someone needs to explain right this second." Cate stood with her arms crossed, one eyebrow raised and a daunting glower on her face. Her pointy-toed shoe tapped an angry staccato on the floor. "But try to use small words so Eric can understand."

At the sound of his name, Eric stopped ogling Rebecca long enough to throw a confused glance in Castor's direction.

"Is this going to take long? My feet are killing me," Florence whined, pulling a chair over and settling noisily into it. She slipped off her shoes and began rubbing her feet, and Maddie waited for her grunts of pleasure to die down before she spoke.

"I know who the killer is."

As soon as the words left her mouth, the group erupted into cacophonous chatter, each exclamation overlapping the others. It was like a nightmare round robin version of the telephone game, played at a decibel level to rival a fire alarm.

"Who is it?"

"How can you be sure? What proof do you have?"

"Do we need to tie them up?"

"Why couldn't you have figured it out three deaths ago?"

"Is it one of us?" They all stared at Eric, who clearly missed the issue with his question. "What?"

"If you'll give me a minute, I'll explain everything." She threw up her hands defensively, revealing the sum total of her evidence. The collectively bewildered response to her major revelation was something of a letdown.

"Did I miss something?" Eric whispered to Rebecca. "What are the grapes for?"

"This is one of a dozen bunches of artificial grapes from the wine cellar," Maddie clarified. "They were part of Helen's décor."

"We're here for a solution to this mystery not a lesson in what to do if you have money but no taste," Castor sneered.

"Well, if not for Helen's bad taste—"

"Astoundingly bad taste, ducks."

"If not for Helen's *astoundingly* bad taste"—she glared at her friend—"the killer might have gotten away with it."

"You've lost me," Florence said. "What do grapes from the wine cellar have to do with the murders? I thought she was strangled."

"She was strangled," Maddie said, feeling almost ninety percent certain she was right. "And I didn't get these from the wine cellar. I got them from the killer's room."

"Why would the killer take a bunch of fake grapes?"

"He didn't. But while the killer was choking the life out of Helen, his dog was engaged in a bit of kleptomania." Time slowed as, one by one, the guests gasped and turned to stare at the killer among them. "I saw these in Ares's dog bed last night during our search and dismissed them as just another dog toy. But today I realized what they really were and that the only way he could have gotten them is if he was present at the time of the murder."

"That's ridiculous," Castor retorted. "He could've snuck down there at any time this weekend. He might have taken them before Helen died."

"Not true," Carlisle interjected. "I locked the door following my inventory, and it remained locked until Helen opened it herself."

"How can you be sure?" Jason asked.

"Because I was under strict orders to ensure that Helen's wishes regarding the wine cellar were respected. I checked the door regularly throughout the day and at the end of the night."

"But we all went into the wine cellar together when we found Helen's body."

"And you held your dog in your arms the entire time," Florence said.

"Still, Ares could have gone down there by himself after the murder," Castor insisted.

"Except that all weekend, he's either been with you or with the big dogs. Mammon and Archer were running with me on Saturday morning, and we kept the dogs out of the wine cellar when we returned for the master key."

"This proves nothing."

"Maybe not, but it's awfully suspicious."

For a long minute Castor stared at Maddie. His mouth opened as if he was about to speak, but no words came out. He was out of quips and excuses. He had no answers or explanations to account for the damning evidence. Defeated, he looked to Ares, who wagged his little tail in joy, oblivious to his inadvertent betrayal. Sadness in his eyes, Castor looked back to his accuser and without warning, he spun toward the front door and dashed from the room.

CHAPTER TWENTY

Stunned, Maddie hesitated just a moment before she followed Castor out the door and down the long hallway. Though, as a runner, she had a clear advantage over him, her momentary stupefaction afforded him a good head start. On top of that, he wasn't wearing a giant windsock and running on a recently waxed floor in shoes with the relative traction of one of Cate's rejuvenating lotions. Still, his escape options were somewhat limited. She felt confident that she would catch him eventually, especially with her considerable entourage.

Following close behind her was Dottie's entire quarter-birthday party in hot pursuit of the man who'd made their lives miserable for the past two days. Their feet clomped on the long hallway floor, an ominous percussion filling the air. In spite of the inevitable arguments, she was relieved to have backup, even in the form of a pack of pampered socialites who were more adept at verbal sparring than any kind of physical altercation. If nothing else, at least there would be a witness to her probable assault.

To their credit, the dogs immediately started running after Castor. Unfortunately, they saw greater joy in trotting back and forth between Castor and his legion of pursuers. Maddie tried to urge them to tackle him or at least grab his pant legs, but every time she called out a command, they came hurtling back toward her, like furry missiles for her to dodge.

Jason popped into her peripheral vision, looking like the poster for a bizarrely fashion-forward action movie as his suit strained against his muscles. He grinned at her, obviously enjoying the chase just a little too much, but she couldn't say she was sad to have him on her side. She glanced to her right, hoping to see his sister—the only other person she expected to keep up with her—but instead she found the least likely candidate keeping pace with her.

"Dottie?"

"Don't be so shocked, pet."

"You hate running. And you're in heels."

"I'm full of surprises."

"That you are," Jason chimed in, inducing a wave of nausea in Maddie.

"And I can do amazing things in heels. Besides, that little weasel ruined my weekend. He has to pay."

Cate pulled up beside them. "I can't believe that lazy bastard actually made a run for it." The small, mincing steps she took to preserve her impractical footwear were entirely unsuited for an all-out chase.

"He's lazy, not stupid," Florence pointed out in spite of her labored breathing.

"I'm not really sure you can call him lazy either. He did kill four people," Eric panted from the rear of the group where he kept Florence company.

"And that redeems him how?" Rebecca snapped.

Like Cate, she was wearing the wrong shoes for the occasion, but she charged ahead anyway. Or at least she tried to but having fallen victim to the perils of a Dottie-supplied wardrobe, her movement was hampered by the combination of heels and a completely alluring though somewhat restricting dress.

"I'm just saying, it does show a certain amount of industriousness," Eric contended between labored breaths.

As the habitual bickering raged on, Maddie attempted to speed up and outrun it, but rather than making any sort of headway, she ended up sliding even more on the glossy hardwood of the long hallway. She probably looked like a cartoon animal running full speed and getting nowhere, and if not for the fact that Castor just escaped out the front door, she would have opted to continue barefoot. Considering the wealth of storm debris littering the ground, she knew she'd regret that action, but at least the fallen branches would slow Castor down as well. All she had to do was make it to the door before she lost him.

She burst through the door and frantically surveyed the surrounding property, hoping to catch a glimpse of her suspect, but there was no trace of him anywhere. He seemed to have disappeared. She didn't know if he had a plan or was simply running blindly. Either way, the situation just got a thousand times worse. Not only was he more familiar with the property than anyone here, but the sun was also beginning its descent. If they didn't catch him before nightfall, his chances of evading capture increased astronomically.

"What do we do now?" Jason looked to her for guidance.

"We have to split up."

"Every time we split up, something bad happens," Florence reminded her. She held her side as she tried to catch her breath.

"Worse than a murderer getting away?" she snapped. "We don't have much choice. He could be anywhere, and we have no idea where he's headed."

"It's the same island we've been stuck on for two days. Where could he possibly go?" Cate folded her arms across her chest and drummed the fingers of her right hand against her left arm.

"It's a large island with countless hiding places, not to mention a boathouse. If there's even a dinghy available to him, he's going to use it to get off this island and get away with murder."

"But he might just as easily be hiding in the bushes by the house," Florence offered an implausible scenario, most likely in consideration of her aversion to running. "We didn't actually see him run away from the house. Someone should probably check the surrounding area, just to be sure."

"Fine. You and Cate can stay here and search through the bushes."

"I'm on bush duty now?" Cate's eyes flashed.

"Would you rather keep running?"

Without another word, Cate picked up a nearby stick, and more haughtily than should have been possible when engaged in such an activity, began jabbing the rhododendrons. Maddie expected she'd find little more than an irritated rabbit for her troubles, but at least she wouldn't have to listen to her complaining.

"Jason, you take Dottie and Carlisle that way." She pointed eastward. "Eric, Rebecca, and I will head in the opposite direction. Hopefully, we'll find him before it gets too dark."

She didn't wait for any of the inevitable objections from the group. They'd already wasted enough time, and she was not about to let Castor get away with murdering four people. She ran full speed in the general direction of the boathouse. Though she couldn't be certain that's where he was headed, she assumed he'd be looking for some way off the island, and she needed to get to him before he utilized it.

The dogs frolicked and crisscrossed in front of her, creating a meandering obstacle course that she absolutely did not need in this moment. Nor did she need the wind that kicked up as she rounded the corner on the west side of the mansion. Under the best of circumstances, it would be difficult to maintain her pace in the face of gale-force winds, but these were far from ideal circumstances. Thanks to her best friend's sartorial sabotage, her dress acted like a parachute on a race car, and with every gust, her billowing sleeves swelled to encumber her further. Assuming they all survived this weekend, she was going to kill Dottie.

Despite the built-in wind resistance of her ensemble, she still managed to leave Eric and Rebecca far behind, and she found herself nearing the boathouse, her only backup the trio of dogs who were currently embroiled in a three-way tug of war with a fallen branch (though in a competition with the larger dogs, tiny Ares ended up being tugged as much as the branch he clung to). She turned around to look for the rest of her help, and saw Eric doubled over and panting. Meanwhile, Rebecca sat on the grass rubbing her ankle and scowling at the broken shoe that dangled from her foot by a strap. They were still several yards away, and though she understood firsthand the perils of confronting a killer alone, she simply couldn't wait. As images of Castor speeding away on a yacht that Helen had named after herself filled her head, she entered the boathouse.

Though she'd seen the structure on her earlier runs, she hadn't entered it until this moment. It was surprisingly unadorned, resembling a cross between a log cabin and a two-car garage with large glass doors that looked out onto the deceptively serene water. In a break from her usual narcissistic interior design, Helen had decorated the space in a classical nautical theme: oars and life preserver rings dotted the walls at regular intervals. A two-seat motorboat occupied one of the boat slips while the other sat empty. In the fading light from the setting sun, Maddie could see that the door to the occupied slip had been dislodged from one of its tracks, most likely by the previous night's violent storms. On the slender wooden dock between the slips, Castor struggled to open the large glass door that stood between him and escape, but it wouldn't budge.

"It's too bad you killed the resident handyman. He might have been able to help you with that." As she closed the distance between them, she kept her eyes on his hands and their proximity to any available weapons.

"I don't suppose you'd lend a hand?"

"I'd rather restrain you."

"Kinky." Even on the verge of being apprehended, he didn't stop making jokes. "But I have something else in mind."

Without warning, he traded his standard smarmy grin for a snarl, like he'd removed a mask to reveal his true face. He lunged for her, and she dodged him.

"You're not going to get away with this, Castor. You can't possibly kill everyone who knows you're guilty." They circled like fighters in a ring.

"You don't know until you try."

He took a swing at her, and she reeled backward, narrowly avoiding the punch. Her evasive maneuver threw her off-balance, however, and after teetering and flailing her arms for the longest few seconds of her life, she tipped backward, falling into the icy water. Saltwater filled her nose and mouth and stung her eyes. She gagged and struggled to reach the surface, but the acres of fabric she wore weighed her down. When she finally popped her head out of the water, she gasped for air, but as soon as she found relief, a strong hand pushed her back under.

She kicked her legs wildly, trying to break free, but the weight of her dress, combined with the pressure from Castor above, was more than a match for her exertions. Her lungs burned, and she fought every impulse to open her mouth for air. In a desperate effort to gain any kind of advantage, she removed her dress. Free of the excess weight that dragged her down, she allowed herself to sink just out of Castor's reach. Then, gathering her remaining strength, she propelled herself back toward the surface, fully expecting to be pushed under once again.

Instead, she met no resistance. She took a full, deep breath, coughed and sputtered and then opened her eyes to find Castor splayed on the dock. All three dogs surrounded him, barking as he held the back of his head and groaned in pain. Above him stood Eric, brandishing one of the decorative oars like a truncheon. As Maddie hoisted herself from the water, Rebecca hobbled in, saw the perilous tableau and immediately hobbled back out to scream for help. Meanwhile Maddie shivered on the dock in her underwear.

Without hesitation, Eric offered her his jacket, solidifying his role as hero. Though she still shivered from the powerful combination of fear, adrenaline and bone-chilling cold coursing through her system, Maddie grabbed two more oars from the walls, and when Rebecca returned, she handed her a weapon and waited for the cavalry to arrive.

"Not that I object, but do you always disrobe while catching killers?" Rebecca asked.

"Only on relaxing weekend getaways," she sighed, hoping that capturing the killer would earn her a get out of jail free card with Dottie. Considering her friend's unnatural love of fashion, she wasn't likely to forgive the untimely demise of the big blue dress anytime soon.

CHAPTER TWENTY-ONE

"You're telling me this Castor fellow killed all those people over money?" Granny asked.

"According to Dottie, he had racked up some astronomical gambling debt and couldn't cover it on his own. He asked his sister to help him out, but she refused."

Maddie had been home over a week, but this was the first chance she'd had to fill her grandmother in on the events of her weekend getaway. As expected, Granny was incredulous, and who could blame her? If she hadn't lived through the experience herself, Maddie wouldn't believe it either.

Granny crossed Maddie's kitchen and set two mugs of coffee on the table near the plate of freshly baked chocolate chip cookies she'd provided. She easily evaded the interested sniffing of Bart and Goliath, who had yet to forgive Maddie for her recent absence. Bart, in particular, clung to his grudge against the injustice of being left with a babysitter (even one he adored), and he excelled at guilt trips. When she'd arrived at Granny Doyle's house to pick them up, he'd looked Maddie in the eye and then turned his back and walked away from her. Of course, his robust resentment hadn't prevented him from claiming his usual spot in the bed and being a complete and total bed hog. Even poor Goliath had been pushed to the outer limits of the mattress, and Maddie rubbed at the knot in her lower back where he'd tap danced on her spine all night.

"What about all the others? Surely he wasn't expecting the hired help to bankroll his bad habit." She scooted the plate of cookies closer to her granddaughter. "I didn't make these for show, young lady. Now eat up."

Obligingly, Maddie helped herself to a still-warm cookie and sighed contentedly after the first delicious bite. "He called them loose ends." She shook her head at the memory of Castor's stolid retelling of events. "Timothy caught him coming out of the wine cellar, so he knew he'd be in trouble once Helen's body was found. He asked Timothy to help him in the teahouse, and once they were far enough from the mansion, Castor murdered him. As for Chef Barbara, she tried to blackmail him."

In truth, she'd tried to blackmail more than one person on the island, a detail that came to light only after Castor revealed the motive behind her death. Apparently, she'd approached Eric first, saying that she had evidence of what he'd done but would keep it quiet for a price. Of course, he was just confused by the whole conversation since everything he'd done had been in full view of the other guests. Unfortunately for Chef Barbara, her discussion with Castor didn't end as well.

"She sounds like a terrible blackmailer."

"But an excellent chef," Maddie said.

"Should have stuck to her strengths, I suppose." Granny patted Goliath's head and offered each of the dogs a treat from her pocket. No wonder Maddie was having difficulty winning back their favor. Perhaps she should line her pockets with steak. "Now, tell me about this Rebecca woman. Is anything developing there?"

"How did you hear about Rebecca?" Maddie asked, though she suspected she knew the answer. She added one more item to her mental list of grievances against Dottie.

"Not from my granddaughter, that's for sure," Granny huffed.

"Because there's not much to tell, Granny." Maddie tried to sidestep the conversation, though she knew she would have to give her something or face endless grilling. Reluctantly, she admitted, "We've been talking." She neglected to mention the frequency of their chats or that they'd been circling the topic of an actual date without the impending threat of death. If her grandmother knew about her nightly calls with Rebecca, Maddie would never hear the end of it.

"Talking? You're never going to get to the good stuff by just talking. You've got to make a move, child."

"I second that bold suggestion, Mrs. Doyle." Dottie swept into the room and helped herself to an aperitif (although, in Dottie's case, the aperitif would likely constitute her meal rather than simply precede it). "And believe me, I have made my opinion on the matter clear."

"And yet that doesn't make the matter less complicated."

"What's complicated about it?" Granny asked. "You like her. She likes you. Get to the kissing already."

Maddie felt a telltale blush creeping up but refused to discuss the matter further with Granny and Dottie. When it came to her love life, they had a singular focus, which excluded pesky considerations like how Maddie felt about the subject. If, for instance, she pointed out how far from Rebecca's league she was, Granny would scold her about her low self-esteem (which was a sure way to boost anyone's ego), and Dottie would harangue her about maintaining a proper beauty regimen. Forget raising other objections like a potential working relationship that could be compromised by a certain-to-fail romance, or Maddie's continued pining for the equally unattainable Officer Murphy. Not that she expected that longing ever to be requited, but it still felt wrong to pursue a romance with one woman while she was secretly yearning for another, which was yet another reason she employed evasive maneuvers whenever Rebecca got too close to actually asking her out. However, she knew all too well that any attempts to discourage them would simply motivate them to try harder. Instead, she changed the subject.

"Did you stop by just to raid my liquor cabinet, or was there another reason for your visit?"

"For your information, this is not a raid, goose. It's a celebration." She approached the table with three tumblers of what appeared to be pure vodka. In a minor miracle, she managed not to spill a drop of alcohol, despite the meniscus of liquid atop each glass.

"What are we celebrating, Dottie?" Granny sipped some of the excess liquid from her glass before she risked lifting it in the air for a toast.

In response, Dottie dramatically waved her left hand between grandmother and granddaughter. There, on her freshly manicured ring finger, a glimmering diamond flashed and sparkled at them. In Dottie's rich history of engagement rings, this was perhaps the least impressive offering, yet she seemed more genuinely thrilled by this development than when she'd snagged her first husband and access to the healthy bank account that came with him.

Maddie leapt from her seat and hugged her tightly, in spite of the nightmare visions of ostentatious bridesmaid dresses already filling her head. If only she could appeal to Jason for a small, simple affair, but she suspected he would readily agree to whatever ludicrous demands Dottie came up with as long as they made her happy. Maddie squeezed her tighter at that thought. When she let go, Granny was right beside her to offer another hug.

"This is cause for celebration. Who's the lucky fella?"

Granny and Maddie sipped at their celebratory drinks while Dottie raved about Jason the entertainment mogul. Having seen and heard all of it before, Maddie tuned out and instead focused on her friend's obvious joy. Nothing was guaranteed with love, especially when Dottie was at the helm, but Maddie thought that, maybe, Jason might be the exception to Dottie's entire marital history. When Dottie poured herself another heavy-handed drink (not twenty minutes after starting the first round), Maddie began making dinner. She couldn't guarantee that anything she prepared would make it into Dottie's stomach, but she knew from past experience that it was better to try than to let her exist on booze alone.

"When did he propose?" Granny asked. She was admiring the ring again, much to Dottie's delight.

"Last night. He said that after our ordeal on the island, he knew he wanted to face life's tribulations with me at his side."

Maddie somehow doubted that Jason had uttered the phrase "life's tribulations," but Dottie-speak aside, it was a sweet sentiment. "I guess your plan worked after all," she said.

"Not in the way I anticipated, but I think we can call the weekend a success, for most of us actually."

"How so?" she asked, keeping a careful eye on the chicken breasts she was sautéing.

She felt sudden pressure on her thigh and looked down to see that both of her dogs were suddenly open to forgiveness, as long as it was bought and paid for in the form of tasty chicken. Not one to waste an opportunity, she slipped them each a small bite, making sure it had cooled first.

"As it happens, Florence has taken over Helen's position with the company, and she's making some significant changes."

"I hope one of them involves being less evil."

"She didn't mention that, but she did say that the company is no longer interested in branching out into the cosmetics industry. As you can imagine, Cate is thrilled."

Considering the certain beauty apocalypse Dottie had forecasted if Helen had gotten her hands on Cate's company, Maddie imagined that her friend was equally ecstatic. She just hoped Cate wouldn't be invited to the wedding.

"In other good news, Mammon, Archer, and Ares have all taken up residence with Helen and Castor's parents. According to my sources, they're loving the good life." Maddie smiled at the thought of her vacation pack staying together. "And Eric is finalizing the purchase of Helen's property."

"I can't believe he still wants to own Murder Island."

"Perhaps he'll have us out for a visit once the renovations are complete."

"I'm busy that weekend," Maddie said. She would rather go pantsless on the Red Line during rush hour than set foot on that island again.

"But Jason and I were considering it as the venue for our nuptials. That place does hold special meaning to our relationship after all."

"Don't take this the wrong way, Dottie, but I'm never traveling with you again."

"Because of a few murders?"

"Because your relaxing weekend getaway almost got me killed."

"Pfft." Dottie waved her bejeweled hand through the air dismissively. "Did you think about the stresses of your daily life even once while we were away?" Maddie refused to acknowledge her friend's all-too-valid point. "Besides, what are the chances anything like that could happen again?"

Aghast, Maddie stared at Dottie, dreading the answer to that question.

www.ingramcontent.com/pod-product-compliance
Lightning Source LLC
Chambersburg PA
CBHW030941310726
48969CB00011B/620